SADIA

SADIA

COLLEEN NELSON

DUNDURN
TORONTO

Cover image: Shutterstock.com/Ungureanu Alexandra
Printer: Webcom

Library and Archives Canada Cataloguing in Publication

Nelson, Colleen, author
    Sadia / Colleen Nelson.

Issued in print and electronic formats.
ISBN 978-1-4597-4029-7 (softcover).--ISBN 978-1-4597-4030-3
(PDF).--ISBN 978-1-4597-4031-0 (EPUB)

    I. Title.

PS8627.E555S23 2018   jC813'.6   C2017-905325-6
                                       C2017-905326-4

1 2 3 4 5   22 21 20 19 18

We acknowledge the support of the **Canada Council for the Arts**, which last year invested $153 million to bring the arts to Canadians throughout the country, and the **Ontario Arts Council** for our publishing program. We also acknowledge the financial support of the **Government of Ontario**, through the **Ontario Book Publishing Tax Credit** and the **Ontario Media Development Corporation**, and the **Government of Canada**.

Nous remercions le **Conseil des arts du Canada** de son soutien. L'an dernier, le Conseil a investi 153 millions de dollars pour mettre de l'art dans la vie des Canadiennes et des Canadiens de tout le pays.

Care has been taken to trace the ownership of copyright material used in this book. The author and the publisher welcome any information enabling them to rectify any references or credits in subsequent editions.

— *J. Kirk Howard, President*

The publisher is not responsible for websites or their content unless they are owned by the publisher.

Printed and bound in Canada.

VISIT US AT

dundurn.com | @dundurnpress | dundurnpress | dundurnpress

Dundurn
3 Church Street, Suite 500
Toronto, Ontario, Canada
M5E 1M2

For Isabella, Evan, and Grace Deeley

CHAPTER 1

After three years of living in Winnipeg, the cold of a February morning still shocked me. My teeth ached from it as I shuffle-walked from Dad's car to the front doors of Laura Secord High School.

I got to my locker as Mariam, my best friend, and the rest of the kids who took the bus stampeded through the front entrance. I was about to call out to her, but something in the way she darted past me — head down, feet moving quickly, as if she didn't want to be seen — made me stop. *Weird*, I thought. We'd been texting each other all weekend. Why would she ignore me?

"Hi, Sadia," Carmina said as she breezed past me. She didn't stop to talk, but headed toward the washroom, lugging her backpack. With a resigned sigh, I realized where Mariam had been going and why she wanted to escape notice. *My* notice.

My fingertips were still numb with cold as I opened my locker and grabbed books for my morning classes. First stop: homeroom. Only grade nine students at LS High School have homeroom. I guess they thought we needed the extra attention. It didn't bother me. I liked my homeroom and I really liked my teacher, Mr. Letner, who taught our Global Issues and English classes.

When I walked into Class 9B, he was already at his desk typing on his computer. Mr. Letner was tall and skinny and had a beard, but was bald, which seemed kind of funny. Like, if he could grow hair on his face, why not his head? I'd been intimidated by him the first day of high school. He had a deep voice and towered over me. But I came to discover that he never yelled; he didn't have to. He was one of those teachers kids were quiet for because most of the time we wanted to hear what he had to say.

"Morning, Sadia! Have a good weekend?" I gave him a weak nod as I sat down at my desk, preoccupied about Mariam. I knew why she'd gone to the washroom. It was to take off her hijab before class started.

"Everything okay?" he asked, zeroing in on me.

"Yeah," I answered, but anyone could tell things weren't okay. I have one of those faces that you can read even if you don't know the alphabet. Big, brown eyes, long lashes, and wide lips that I can squeeze and squish into a hundred different positions. Rubber lips, Dad calls them. I sunk lower in my seat and kept my eyes fixed on the desk ahead of me, corners of my lips turned down. I might even have sighed.

There was no point in talking about it to Mr. Letner; there was nothing he could do. Mariam had mentioned de-jabbing a while ago. I'd assumed it was just talk, but then one day before winter break, she'd gone to the washroom with Carmina and come back without her head scarf. I'd stared at her long hair and uncovered head. She looked so *bare*. The hijab was distracting, she'd told me, and she needed to concentrate for the test we were having that morning. A hundred warnings rang in my head.

Since that day, she'd been taking the head scarf off more and more often. Egyptian, Mariam had large, green eyes, wide cheekbones, and skin a shade darker than mine. She complained about her nose, saying it was too big and she wished it were straight and narrow like mine, but she was just being dramatic. Her nose was fine. Without her hijab, she'd toss her hair over her shoulder and throw looks at me that said I should ditch my hijab, too. I'd thought about it — how could I not? We went to a school where only a handful of girls wore hijab. It *would* be easy to look like everyone else.

But that wasn't how I'd been raised, and neither had Mariam. Islam was clear: females, once they were old enough, should dress modestly. And for our families, that meant keeping everything but our faces, hands, and feet covered. I hoped de-jabbing was just a phase for her, something she was testing out.

I looked up as Mariam walked into the class with Carmina. Today, not only had she taken off her hijab, she'd also changed out of the long tunic top she usually wore and put on a tight T-shirt. I recognized it as one of Carmina's; *Hollister* was splashed across the front in curvy writing. I kept my eyes down, trying to ignore her outfit. I could almost feel her waiting for me to say something, but I didn't want to give her the satisfaction. If she was de-jabbing for attention, she'd have to get it from someone else.

"Hey!" Carmina said, drawing the word out and flashing me a glossy-lipped smile. Carmina is Filipino and has dark hair that hangs straight and shiny; she's a shampoo commercial come to life. Even though she was aiding and abetting the de-jabbing, I wasn't mad at her; she didn't get why Mariam changing out of her normal clothes was a big deal. But Mariam did.

Mom had warned me about things like this. She'd sat me down before I started high school and told me that I might want to do things like Mariam was doing now. But she said it was up to me to make the right choice. I'd nodded. She'd also said it can be hard living in a place like Canada where so many people have different beliefs, but that was why they had picked it as our new home — because Canada was a place that accepted differences.

We'd left Syria just before things went haywire. Most of our relatives had already moved to the U.K., so we'd gone there first and stayed with family while we waited for our Canadian visas to come through. The position Dad had accepted at the University of Manitoba meant we'd be moving to a place we knew nothing about.

When I thought back to those first months in Canada, it made me cringe. I didn't know *anything* compared to now. After the first day of school, my older brother, Aazim, had picked me up from school and held my hand on the walk home even though I was twelve and he was fifteen. I complained about missing my friends and living in a place where I couldn't understand what people said. His first day of school had probably been just as awkward as mine, but instead of complaining, he comforted me, reassuring me things would get better. He was right, of course, but there had been some difficult days at the beginning.

The transition for Dad had been easier. He'd learned English in the U.K. as a university student and spoke with a British accent that he was slowly losing the longer we lived in Canada. Mom's English wasn't as good as Dad's, but she worked at it every day, going to classes at the language centre and joining conversational English groups. She took it as a challenge to master a language that had nothing in common with Arabic. I knew it was her dream to work again.

In Syria, she'd been the head librarian at Damascus University. She and Dad would walk to work together after they saw us off to school. But in Canada, things changed. She became a stay-at-home mom, taking the bus to do her shopping and looking after our house. She called her parents and sisters often, FaceTiming them at their flats in England. When we went to the public library, she gazed longingly at the shelves of books, watching the librarians go about their work with hawk-ish interest.

Since we'd left Syria, I'd become more Canadian than I would have thought possible. With barely a trace of an accent, I was a top student. My memories of Syria were tucked in a shoebox under my bed, the connection to my home country fading year by year. I cast a quick glance at Mariam. Carmina passed her a tube of pink lip gloss, which she smeared across her lips. She turned to me, her lips shining like they'd been lacquered. "What?" she asked. It was a challenge; I could see it in the arch of her eyebrow.

"Nothing," I replied, frowning at the thought of what her parents would do if they found out how she was dressing at school.

"Okay, everyone, get settled," Mr. Letner called. "'O Canada' is going to start in a minute." There was the usual foot dragging as people got to their seats and slapped binders onto desks.

The bell that signalled the start of morning classes rang and today's student announcer said, "Please stand for the singing of 'O Canada.'"

Beside me, Mariam whispered, "It's Josh!" I gave her a quizzical look. "On the announcements," she explained, giddily. I had to bite my tongue. Since when was hearing Josh Jensen on the announcements a big deal? As the music started, Carmina gave Mariam a conspiratorial smile that could only mean one thing.

It was news to me that Mariam liked Josh. I mean, he was funny, smart, super-athletic, and cute. He had brown eyes and blond hair, shaved short on the sides and left longer on top so it swooped down over his forehead. Tons of girls had crushes on him; I saw them drooling over him all the time. But Mariam and Josh had nothing in common. It would make sense if *I* had a crush on Josh, and if I was being honest, maybe I did a little. We both liked sports, had been the student council sports reps last year, and ran intramurals at our middle school. Watching Mariam's bright-eyed smile as Josh spoke gave me an unexpected pang of jealousy. What if he liked her back? I took a deep breath and forced myself to relax. What did it matter? Neither of us could date him.

Josh made some announcements about upcoming school events and then said, "Tryouts for the Junior Varsity All-City Pre-Season Basketball Tournament start today in the gym at lunch. It's a co-ed team, so any-one in grade nine or ten is welcome to try out."

I perked up. Mr. Letner was coaching the tourna-ment team this year and had given us a heads-up about tryouts. Making the co-ed team meant I would be a shoe-in for the school's JV girls team, even though I was only grade nine.

I was the only girl in hijab I knew who played bas-ketball. I blamed my brother. When we moved into our house in Winnipeg, he spent hours outside shooting hoops. Mom got sick of me watching from the window and shooed me outside to join him. It wasn't just that I liked spending time with my brother, it was the *swish* of the net when a shot went in and the quick rhythm of the ball against the pavement. I liked being on my toes, anticipating Aazim's next move, like in a fast-moving chess game. I wasn't as good as Aazim, but I could do a crossover that rivalled his. I was quick and gave him a run for his money when we played one on one. My last birthday, Aazim got me a poster of my favourite player, Kyle Lowry of the Toronto Raptors, and Dad bought me a pair of real basketball shoes: black-and-turquoise high-tops with Michael Jordan's silhouette on the side.

When Josh walked into class after he'd finished the announcements, Mariam tracked his progress down the aisle to his desk beside Allan. I didn't understand where her sudden interest in Josh had come from. It had prac-tically sprung up overnight, and I wondered if he was the reason for the clothes and the lip gloss. Carmina had a crush on a guy named Daniel in grade ten who she talked about *all the time,* even though she'd never actually had a conversation with him. Carmina had always been more interested in boys than Mariam and me, but lately, her obsession with having a boyfriend had reached a new high. I found it nauseating, but clearly Mariam didn't. In fact, it looked like it had rubbed off on her.

As Mariam watched Josh sit down, I read the word Mr. Letner had written on the board: *Perspective.*

"Anyone want to tell me what that word means?" he asked. A few kids were on their phones, not paying attention. He paused, staring at them until they realized and put them away.

"Like in art, it shows how near or far something is," Carmina said.

"You can lose it," Allan offered. "As in, 'I'm losing perspective.'" There were snickers from a few kids. Allan was Josh's best friend, but unlike Josh, Allan was a jerk and thought it was funny to make up rude nicknames for people and burp so loud he was sent to the office for disrupting class. Josh kept trying to assure me that underneath all the rude behaviour, Allan was a good guy, but I didn't see it.

Mr. Letner gave a reluctant nod, but I could tell he was looking for something else. He narrowed his eyes at us, as if he could send the answer telepathically.

"Point of view," Riley said quietly. He sat at the back and didn't usually say much, not because he wasn't smart, he was just really shy.

"Right!" Mr. Letner jumped off the table he was perched on and went to his computer. "Understanding what perspective is will be essential to completing this new project."

There were a few groans, but not from me. *Good,* I thought, *something to take my mind off Mariam and the smell of her cherry lip gloss.* Mr. Letner turned on the Smartboard at the front of the class and a website appeared. "'If You Give a Kid a Camera,'" he read. "Anyone heard of this before?" No one put up their hand. "Anyone heard of the picture book *If You Give a Mouse a Cookie*? Your parents might have read it to you when you were little." I hadn't, but when I looked around the room, a lot of kids had their hands up.

Mr. Letner went to his desk and picked up a book with a mouse in overalls on the cover. "It's one of my kid's favourites," he said. "'If you give a mouse a cookie, he's going to ask for a glass of —'" He broke off and a bunch of kids finished the sentence with "Milk." Mr. Letner turned the page. "'If you give a mouse some milk, he'll probably ask you for a —'"

"Straw." Mr. Letner nodded and put the book on his desk. "You get the idea."

I didn't get it. I frowned at him. I wanted him to explain about the book! How would I understand the assignment if I didn't know what everyone else did!

Mr. Letner pointed to the Smartboard. "I want to show you this project that a teacher started in India. She wanted to give kids living in poverty a chance to tell their stories. It's called If You Give a Kid a Camera. What do you think would happen if you got cameras?"

"Duh, we'd take pictures?" Allan suggested sarcastically.

"Hopefully," Mr. Letner replied, frowning at Allan's rudeness. "And if you take pictures —"

"We'll want to share them?"

"And if you share them …"

There was a pause as everyone thought about it.

"We'll show people how we see the world." This time the answer came from Josh.

"Yes!" Sometimes Mr. Letner put his finger to his nose and pointed at the person who gave the right answer. He did this for Josh, which made Josh grin. "Perspective! Understanding global issues, like poverty and war and the environment, is all about *perspective.* The If You Give a Kid a Camera project was such a success in India that it has spread to other developing countries: Brazil, Sudan, Thailand. Kids around the world were empowered to share their stories through their photos." He gave a dramatic pause and looked out at all of us, then pulled a hard plastic case from under his desk. "I've got twenty-eight digital cameras for you to use for the next few weeks. It's going to be a bit of an experiment to see what images you capture. I want you to take photos of the things that matter to you, moments that you want to share with us. Not posed photos, but real life. I want you to notice things you haven't noticed before, take a fresh look at things, and present photos that show life from your perspective."

There was a chorus of complaints.

"*Another* project?"

"We just got a big assignment in bio, too."

"How many marks is it worth?"

Mr. Letner didn't let anybody derail him. He moved around the class handing out the outline for the project. The title in bold letters read: "If You Give a Kid a

Camera." The marking guide was below. It was worth 40 percent of our final grade! I raised my eyebrows at him and pointed it out to Mariam.

"Can't we just use our phones?" Carmina asked. She was addicted to Instagram and Snapchat.

"No." Mr. Letner shook his head. "And try not to let this become a selfie bonanza. There is more to photograph in the world than just your faces." He sort of grimaced when he said the last part. "I want all the photos saved on the memory card inside the camera." He pulled a square piece of plastic out of one of the cameras and held it up.

Mr. Letner changed the screen from the home page of If You Give a Kid a Camera to show us the young photographers and the pictures they'd taken. We all sat silently as he clicked through. Based on what we'd discussed in Global Issues about poverty in developing countries, I expected to see kids in shacks or playing in a garbage pile or standing by a well with a leaky tap.

But the photos that flashed on the screen showed kids playing soccer and splashing in puddles. There were some pictures of kids with invented toys and playing in a band of instruments created out of garbage. In most of the pictures, the kids were laughing. Despite the living conditions, the photographers focused on the joy in their lives, not the hardship.

Mr. Letner brought the screen back to the home page. "The kids who got the cameras showed us what life was like from their perspective. They used it as a communication tool, and as we know, a lot of global issues can be solved through understanding."

"I can't believe you're trusting us with cameras," Zander said.

"Funny you should say that, because I'm not. A form was emailed home today letting your parents know about our project. The cameras cost two hundred dollars, so if they're lost or damaged, you're on the hook for the cost. We'll post some of the photos on the blog, so make sure they are appropriate." He gave Allan a pointed look. All the grade nine homerooms had a blog for students to keep track of assignments.

As part of our class mark, we also had to sign up to write a post each term. I'd written one in first term about Ramadan, the holiest month of the Islamic calendar. Kids at school couldn't believe I fasted every day for a month. As weird as it sounded to them, I liked fasting. A little discomfort at school meant a big payoff at home. Mom spent the day in the kitchen, cooking food for when we broke the fast each night at sundown. Last year, to mark the end of the fasting period, Mariam's family had joined us for Eid al-Fitr, and we all ate together. It had been my favourite Eid since we'd moved to Canada.

"Do we get the cameras today?"

"Your parents have to email the form back to me and then you can take them home."

Despite the complaints from other kids, a lot of ideas about what I could photograph ran through my head. Basketball, to start with, my runners, some of Mom's *rizz bi halib,* the best creamy sweet toast ever!

"This is stupid," Mariam mumbled beside me. I thought she'd be excited about the project.

"I think it sounds fun," Carmina said.

"Me, too."

"There's nothing cool in my life," Mariam replied. "It'll just be a bunch of boring pictures of me at home. My parents don't let me *do* anything," she whined.

"You like to sew. Maybe you could take pictures of some of the stuff you've been making?" Mariam shot me a look like I didn't know what I was talking about. I tried not to let it bother me, but between the de-jabbing and the attitude, I didn't need a new perspective to see that Mariam was pushing me away. What I didn't know was why.

CHAPTER 2

I ate my lunch so quickly I was finished before most kids had unpacked their sandwich. "What's the rush?" Mariam asked. She lazily opened a container of leftovers: rice and lentils in curry that she'd heated in the microwave. The smell wafted over and I took a second to enjoy it. Mariam's mom was a really good cook. Going to her house for dinner was like eating at a gourmet Egyptian restaurant.

"Basketball tryouts," I told her, sucking the last drops out of my juice box. The carton crumpled in my hands.

Mariam looked at Carmina and grimaced. She'd played basketball last year when we were in middle school, but not with much enthusiasm. I think she gave up before the season finished.

"Why would you want to play basketball, anyway?" Mariam asked. She looked at Carmina, who was staring across the cafeteria at her grade ten crush.

"Why *wouldn't* you?" I shot back.

"Boys don't like girls who play sports."

I held my tongue, sure that if I said anything, I'd regret it. Then I stuffed my lunch containers back in my bag and stood up. "Whatever. I'm going. See you."

I didn't look back, but I'm pretty sure I heard her and Carmina giggling as I walked away.

When I got to the gym, it was almost all boys. "You're here early," Josh said as I went past him to the girls' change room. He was sitting on a bench, tying his shoes. New white-and-silver Air Jordans.

"So are you."

"Got to get a jump on the competition," he said with a sly grin.

Josh stood up and jogged over to a wire basket of balls Mr. Letner had put out for us. He picked one and dribbled it, then ran past me and did a layup. I laughed to myself. If Mariam *really* liked Josh, she'd know this was where she needed to be.

I walked into the change room. The other girls were getting changed into shorts and T-shirts. I went into a stall and took off my regular outfit — long pants and long-sleeved shirt — to put on my sweats and a different long-sleeved shirt. The head scarf had to stay on, and when I came out of the stall, I took a quick look in the mirror and then found a spot on a bench to put on my basketball shoes. Being in there gave me a minute to get focused and concentrate on what I had to do to make the tournament team.

More girls came in and I did a quick head count. There were eight of us trying out and there would probably be about twenty boys. Mr. Letner said he'd take a team of twelve to the tournament, but the rules were that at least a quarter of the team had to be girls. That meant at least three girls would make it. I said a quick prayer that one of the three would be me.

Most of the boys were already bouncing balls and taking shots on net when I got to the gym. My stomach did a flip and my fingers tingled. I couldn't wait to feel the bumpy rubber of the ball and the slap as it hit the floor and bounced back into my hands. Mr. Letner blew his whistle. The thumping of balls stopped and we hustled toward him. I grabbed a ball and held it against my waist.

"Okay, everyone," Mr. Letner said. "We'll start with some shooting drills. Girls on one side and boys on the other. Then we'll do some one on one. Ready?" He blew his whistle again and I ran to the hoop and took my first shot. It went in with a swish, which I thought was a good sign.

"Nice one," a voice piped up behind me. Jillian Triggs sent her shot sailing through the air and it went in, too.

We took our spot in line and waited for another turn. "Which guys do you think will make it?" Jillian asked. She wasn't in Mr. Letner's class and hadn't gone to my middle school, so I didn't know her well. She was a head taller than me, and I could see her fluorescent pink sports bra peeking out from under her tank top. "Josh, Rory, Thomas, Lukas … and maybe Allan," I added as he missed his shot from the free-throw line to a lot of jeering. "But after that, they're all kind of the same."

"Yeah. Mohammed's pretty good, too. He's on my street and we play together in the summer sometimes."

It was my turn again, so I dribbled the ball and took another shot. It bounced off the rim and back to me. I shot again. This time, it went in.

Mr. Letner wandered over with his clipboard. "Okay, girls. Show me what you can do." Jillian took a shot that arced into the air and through the net like she'd buttered it. Mr. Letner whistled in appreciation. "Let's play some one on one. Who's up first?" My hand went up and I looked over at Jillian, who had also raised her hand, and grinned. "You two," Mr. Letner said. Jillian rolled her ball to the wall and I took my spot at the top of the key. Jillian crouched down, her ponytail swinging over one shoulder. I slapped the ball and dribbled it a few times, turning my body to guard it. Jillian moved in, swiped for it, but I dodged her, driving up the left, and took a shot. It went in and I bit back a smile. My runners squeaked as I ran back to the top of the key. Jillian had the ball, but this time she drove right. I had my hands up, jumping to block her. My arm caught my hijab, which was loose after all the running and jumping. It fell over my eye and I was distracted. Jillian saw her moment and moved past me easily. She took her shot as I stopped to fix my scarf.

Mr. Letner blew his whistle. "Okay, Sadia?"

"Yes," I groaned, frustrated. It was like having to stop to tie a shoelace.

"Next two girls, you're up."

My hair kept leaking out of the bonnet cap underneath my head scarf. I had to move to the side to fix it. The first time I'd worn a hijab, it had taken me five minutes to get it on my head properly. Now, I could fix it without looking in a mirror in a less than a minute. But not in the middle of the gym!

Mom and Dad had agreed I'd start wearing hijab when I turned thirteen. The first day of grade eight, Mariam and I had walked into school with the head covering and people had given us funny looks. They didn't know hijab had always been in our future, so I guess they were surprised. I was glad that Mariam had started wearing her hijab at the same time. It made it easier having her beside me. I was proud of the hijab and of what it meant; that I was choosing to be modest. A lot of people thought that I covered myself to avoid a man's gaze, but it was more than that. It was a way to express my spiritual connection to God, and it was how I had been raised.

But still, walking into my middle school wearing hijab that first day had been nerve-racking. I'd left grade seven as a tomboy, playing soccer at lunch with the boys, but I came back covered up and feeling older, more mature. None of the kids asked any questions, but I saw them looking at Mariam and me as if they weren't sure we were the same people. I didn't play soccer at lunch that day, worried that I'd mess up my hijab and not be able to put it back on properly. Instead, Mariam and I had stayed in the cafeteria. But when I'd seen the boys come in, sweaty and red-faced after lunch, Josh bragging that he'd scored two goals, my insides had twisted. Just because I wore hijab didn't change who I was on the inside. The next day, I left Mariam at our cafeteria table with Carmina. I went outside and hung around the goalposts, waiting for the boys to notice me. When the ball was kicked out of bounds, I got to it first. "Are you playing?" Josh asked, running up beside me.

"Whose team am I on?"

"We get Sadia!" he shouted out. I lifted the ball over my head, tossed it to Josh, and ran into the game. After that, it was like nothing had changed.

My hijab didn't bother me so much when I was playing sports outside. The rules were loose and everyone else had on their school clothes. But it was a hindrance now, when I was trying out for a team and everyone else was in their gym clothes. Sudden movements and running could make it slip out of place.

I gave a frustrated groan as I felt the scarf slide farther back and had to stop to fix it, again. "Do you have to wear that?" Jillian asked, coming up beside me.

"Yeah," I said. "I can't take it off, especially here." Did she understand what I meant by *here*? In public, with a lot of people around, especially males who weren't my family?

"It must be such a pain." I was about to argue that it wasn't, but who was I kidding? I couldn't take a jump shot without the bottom of the scarf flying in my face. It wasn't like it was my first time playing wearing hijab, but I needed to do more than just play to make the team. I needed to *bring it.*

"And aren't you hot?" She stuck out her tongue like a dog panting. "I'm sweating and I'm wearing shorts and a tank top." I looked down at my black sweatpants and shirt that covered my arms, all the way to my wrists.

"Yeah," I admitted. Hot and irritated.

Mr. Letner blew his whistle. "Scrimmage time!" Everyone put their balls into the wire bin by the equipment room and met in the middle of the gym. Mr. Letner numbered us off: "One, two, one, two." Allan kept dodging his turn to be counted until he was sure to get a number one, which was Josh's team. I was number one, too, but Jillian was on the other team and so were a lot of the really good players. It looked like the teams were lopsided, but Josh didn't care. He called a quick team huddle, assuming the role of team captain.

"Sadia, you're small forward. Allan, point guard. I'll play power forward." He pointed to the other kids, assigning them positions. I looked at Jillian's team, where she was doing the same thing. We all put our hands into the middle of the circle and shouted, "Three, two, one, Thunder!" at the same time. Half the kids went to sit on the bench, waiting to be rotated in, and the other five of us took our spots on court.

Jillian was centre and towered over Abby, the girl Josh had picked for the position. Abby was long limbed, but didn't move quickly. Jillian got past her and threw the ball upcourt. Josh intercepted it and the play switched toward our zone. "Josh!" I called for the ball, holding my hands up. Mohammed got in my face, but I dodged and caught the pass from Josh, drove to the net, and scored. Josh came running at me for a high-five. The scrimmage kept going like that for the next twenty minutes. Every two minutes, we subbed in new players, but my heart was racing each time I took a break on the bench. Beads of sweat popped out on my forehead, and I wished I could have played in shorts like the other kids, or even just a short-sleeved shirt!

Josh and I ran on again for the last shift. We'd just scored and the point guard on Jillian's team, Thomas, slapped the ball to put it in bounds. We all ran upcourt, ready to defend their press. Thomas was trying to toss the ball to Jillian, but we'd boxed her in and she couldn't dart away. As the ball flew through the air, I jumped up and tipped it out of her hands. I didn't see Abby's elbow — my hijab blocked vision on my right side. The bone came down hard on my nose, and I felt a warm spurt of blood on my upper lip.

Mr. Letner blew his whistle and the game stopped. I cupped my hand over my nose and mouth. "Whoa! Whoa! Sadia, you okay?"

I nodded, but kept my head down. A few drops of dark red blood dotted the gym floor. "I'll get an ice pack," Jillian said and raced to the gym office. Josh took my arm and led me to the bench. Mr. Letner handed me a wad of tissues.

"At least we'll get a free throw," Josh said, trying to find the silver lining.

My nose throbbed. I knew that if my hijab hadn't been in my way, I would have been able to see Abby's elbow coming down and could have ducked.

"What happened?" Mariam asked when I came back to class. I'd been sitting in the office, waiting for the bleeding to stop. She had probably heard from other kids, but it was nice to see her concerned.

"I got hit in the face. I'm okay." Every time I scrunched up my face, it felt hot and tingly.

"It looks kind of swollen."

I gingerly touched the skin on either side of my nose. "Yeah. I hope it's not broken."

"And *that* is why I don't play sports."

I wanted to roll my eyes at her so badly, but I restrained myself. I didn't know why she was acting like this. Did she really think sports were dumb?

I'd always been the sporty one, even though Mariam had three brothers and I only had one. She'd never understood why I'd rather play soccer at recess than sit on a bench and talk, but we had so many other things in common, that it didn't used to matter.

Used to.

Mariam had arrived a year before me. Even if we hadn't both been Muslim and attended the same mosque, we would have been friends. We used to stay up late watching movies and talking. She was so easy to be around and always had some new idea to try, like ambushing Aazim with water guns when he came home from school or baking cookies for the school bake sale. I missed that Mariam.

And it wasn't like her friendship with Carmina was new, either. Carmina had always been our third — like, if we had to do a project with three people, she was the one we asked. We all ate lunch together and hung out after school, but lately, I'd noticed I was becoming the third. The two of them were doing things together while I was on the periphery.

"How's the nose?" Josh asked as we packed up our books at the end of the day.

"I'll live," I said and tried to wiggle it to prove it to him.

"So, you and Josh were on the same team?" Mariam asked after he'd walked away. She pulled out the head scarf and tunic she'd stuffed into her locker. I walked with her to the washroom so she could change and we could catch the bus home. I nodded. "Did he ask you to be on his team or, like, what happened?"

"Mr. Letner chose the teams. It was a close game, too. We could have won if I hadn't gotten hurt."

Mariam pushed open the door to the girls' washroom. We were the only ones in there, and in a few minutes, she'd slipped her tunic over her T-shirt and had her hair tucked under the stretchy bonnet cap. Her scarf was fuchsia pink and it made her skin glow. The ends were embroidered with white thread. "That's really pretty," I said, admiring it.

Mariam sighed and tossed an end over her shoulder. "If I have to wear it, it can at least be stylish." She gave my hastily chosen hijab, as boring-beige as it could get, a pitiful look. I shrugged it off. Fashion had never been my thing. "Come on, we're going to miss our bus," she added.

Because I was waiting for you were the words I wanted to say, but I bit my tongue. Again.

CHAPTER 3

"Did you reply to Mr. Letner's email about taking a camera home?" I asked my mom at dinner. She'd made one of Dad's favourite meals, a spicy chicken dish, and our lips and fingers shone with grease.

"Yes," she replied. "He's an interesting teacher. Always with a new idea. You like his class?"

I nodded. "He wants us to take photos," I explained to Dad. "About how we see the world."

Aazim grinned at me. "The only thing you see is the basketball court."

Since he'd started university, Aazim hadn't been around as much as he used to be. He said he preferred to study at school, where it was quiet, as if the three of us were loud, rambunctious five-year-olds. "Not the only thing," I said defensively.

He scoffed, wiping his fingers on a paper towel and leaving greasy smudges behind. "Your days of playing basketball are numbered, little sister."

"No!"

"You'll have to stop being a tomboy and become a dutiful Muslim woman, right?" He was teasing — we both knew our parents were fine with me playing sports. I kicked his shin under the table and he winced.

"Stop it, you two," Dad said, raising an eyebrow and throwing Aazim and me a warning look that we knew better than to test. Dad's skin was darker than mine or Mom's, and when he did yardwork in the summer, it tanned a deep brown. His thick, curly black hair was unruly and always looked like it needed a cut.

"The email from Mr. Letner said you are supposed to take photos of things that matter to you. There's more than just basketball. You should show your classmates what your life is like. It might be interesting for them." I knew what Mom meant by *life*. She meant being Muslim. From the kitchen, I could see the small prayer mat in front of the window in the dining room. Mom used it five times a day for her prayers. Now that I was older, I'd started using it for my prayers, too. The mat had come with us from Syria and was soft from use. Dad had one in the bedroom, where he preferred to pray. He had one at his office, too.

I doubted kids at school would be interested in that, but instead of disagreeing with her, I gave a noncommittal shrug.

"Did you get your sociology exam back?" Dad asked Aazim.

Aazim shook his head. He attended the same university where Dad taught, but they rarely bumped into each other. Dad was an economics professor and spent his time in the Arts building, while Aazim was pre-med, according to my parents, or first year science, according to him. The one arts course Aazim had to take was

Sociology, but he'd scheduled it to avoid bumping into Dad. "I saw you going into the Isbister Building today. I didn't think you had any courses there."

And *that* was the reason Aazim had carefully planned the location of his classes. Dad's interest in his life was well meaning, but I knew it wore on Aazim.

"I don't," Aazim said with a frown. "Why were *you* there?" he added.

"I had a department meeting. We use the board-room in that building." I still wasn't totally clear on what economics was. Dad said he sat around all day in his office, writing research papers. Sometimes, he'd teach a course if they let him. He was joking. I'd seen the letters and emails from students thanking him for being a great teacher. Dad loved to tell stories, and I had no doubt that he was able to entertain his students the same way he entertained Aazim and me. When we were kids, he didn't read us bedtime stories, he told us tales that he'd been told by his father. A great actor, he had a different voice for each character and would play out the most exciting scenes, leaping from the bed to the floor until he had Aazim and me gripping the covers and barely breathing.

"I was just meeting some friends," Aazim said, wiping his fingers again and leaving more greasy streaks behind. "Did you do anything today?" he asked Mom.

"Went to the grocery store, cooked, cleaned. The usual." Mom sighed. "Although, I did see something interesting in the newspaper. The Millennium Library downtown is starting an Arabic section. There are a lot more Arabic speakers in the city now."

"Maybe they'll need a librarian?" I suggested.

"Maybe," she said, although she sounded doubtful.

"Did you get any marks back?" Dad asked turning to me. Most of our dinner conversation centred around school: upcoming tests, studying for tests, and marks from tests. "No, but the tryouts for the tournament team started today."

"Back to basketball," Aazim mumbled.

"How did they go?" Mom asked. I saw tension flash on her face. Playing on a co-ed team was a bit of a tricky thing for us now that I was older. I knew they'd feel better once I was playing for an all-girls team, but making the tournament team was a big deal and I'd been excited when they'd agreed to let me try out.

"Fine, until I was hit in the face." Everyone looked at me. I'd actually forgotten about it by the time I came home from school. The pain was gone, but my nose still felt swollen when I scrunched it up.

"What happened?" Mom peered at me. She wore wire-rimmed glasses that made her look even more like a librarian. Thin and tall, she had light brown eyes and wore a serious expression, like she was always thinking about something.

"A girl elbowed me in the nose. It was an accident. We were both going for the ball. It was bleeding, though, and I had to sit in the office for a while until it stopped."

"Hmm. Maybe the game is too rough."

I shook my head quickly. "It was my fault. I wasn't paying attention. My scarf got in my face."

My parents glanced at each other across the table. I held my breath. The last thing I needed was for them to decide basketball was too dangerous and tell me I couldn't try out.

"Her nose wasn't that great, anyway," Aazim said. I gave him another kick to the shins as Mom and Dad laughed. Thanks to Aazim's *hilarious* sense of humour, the matter of basketball being too dangerous was dropped.

CHAPTER 4

I had just sat down in homeroom when I heard my name over the school PA system.

"Sadia Ahmadi, please come to the office. Sadia Ahmadi." The secretary's voice cut through the morning chatter in the classroom. Mr. Letner nodded for me to go. "O Canada" hadn't been played yet and, once again, Mariam was with Carmina switching outfits in the washroom.

"Are you Sadia?" Mrs. Mooney, the secretary, asked as she looked up from her computer. I nodded. "Have a seat." I sat down in a chair opposite her desk. "Mrs. Marino will be with you in a minute."

The door to the vice-principal's office opened and I could hear her speaking slowly and clearly, annunciating every word. A girl in a hijab, head down, emerged first, followed by her parents. They were smiling and nodding vigorously, nudging their daughter to show more enthusiasm for what Mrs. Marino was saying. The girl looked at me, and for a second, a wave of relief washed over her, but then she turned away and took a step closer to her parents.

Mrs. Marino had voluminous, curly hair. It looked like it weighed the same as she did and I wondered how she didn't topple over from it. "Sadia, this is Amira Nasser. A new student. She's starting today." I smiled at Amira when she glanced up, but she didn't return it. I took in her clothes and what her parents were wearing. On my first day of school, Mom had made me wear my best outfit: a dress and party shoes. I'd felt ridiculous when everyone else was in jeans or leggings. The next day, I'd worn jeans and runners, like I would have at home. Amira's clothes weren't fancy. I turned my gaze to her parents. Her mom kept nodding, even though no one was saying anything, and she gave me an enthusiastic smile, which didn't match the dark circles under her eyes. It was like she was trying so hard to be happy, it was exhausting her.

"The Nassers are from Syria," Mrs. Marino said. A brief, knowing glance passed between her and Mrs. Mooney. I caught the look of pity on their faces, but wasn't sure if the Nassers saw it, too.

Mom and Dad hadn't shielded me from the news. I knew what was happening in Syria. I'd seen the footage of buildings being blown up and refugees walking across Europe, hoping to find a safe place for their family. There was a war in my home country. Mom and Dad had been glued to the internet since the first reports started to surface a few years ago. They muttered and shook their heads as places they knew, places we'd visited, were reduced to rubble. And then the reports started showing refugees leaving. Desperate to escape the country, they'd cross the Mediterranean Sea in rowboats or inflatable dinghies.

The footage on the screen wasn't the Syria I remembered. It looked like another planet. The eyes of the children were haunted, their clothes and bodies dirty and unwashed because there was no water. Some towns were cut off from food supplies, and the children were starving. Then, one day, I'd turned away from the news, not wanting to have my happy memories of Syria replaced with these ugly ones. I'd grabbed my jacket to go outside and play basketball, comforted by the rhythmic bounce of the ball on concrete. But Mom had forced me to sit it out. "Watch," she'd said, "and be thankful. That could be you."

Before we left Damascus, I'd seen people beaten on the street, twice. The first time, I was in our house and heard an uproar outside. I went to the balcony overlooking the street and saw our neighbour, Mr. Habib, being yelled at by two officers with machine guns slung over their shoulders. He held up his hands, shrinking away from them, but they pulled out batons and began hitting him. Even when he was on the ground, they kept kicking him, and then they dragged him into a van. Mom pulled me away from our balcony, scolding me for risking my safety. "Don't draw attention to yourself!" she'd hissed at me. All my life, she'd told me to stick up for myself, not to let anyone put me down, and now she was saying I should hide? I stared at her in confusion.

The second time, I was returning from a shopping trip with Teta, my grandmother. A ruckus broke out on the street. I moved through the crowd to see what was happening. A group of men were shouting at a man and his teenage son, accusing them of being traitors. The onlookers jeered, tossing rocks at them. One hit the boy and made him bleed. He clung to his father, crying with fear. Sitta dragged me away, shouting at me the whole way home that I had to be more careful. When we got home and Sitta told my parents what had happened, Dad said he'd had it. I didn't know what he meant, but he stayed up late for weeks, talking on the phone and making arrangements. His friends thought he was crazy for leaving; he had arguments with them and sometimes they'd storm out of our house, furious. But Mom and Dad thought it was going to get worse before it got better. Luckily for us, we already had family in the U.K., so it made leaving easier. I wondered sometimes about the people who thought Dad was crazy. Were they still there? Had they left, too? Or were some of them the haunted faces we saw on the news?

Amira's parents pushed her toward me, smiling encouragement. "Hi," I said in English.

She stared at me.

"*Marhaba*," I tried again in Arabic. She nodded, her hands fidgeting at her sides. She'd brought no backpack or binders.

"Can you show Amira around, Sadia? She'll have the same timetable as you, except she's taking art instead of band. Mr. Letner will be her homeroom teacher as well," Mrs. Marino said. It was horrible but my first thought was no. I didn't want this sad, haunted girl with me. She'd follow me around like a lost puppy. I hated myself for thinking that way and pushed those thoughts away.

"Sure," I answered. Mrs. Marino held out her hand to shake Amira's parents' hands. I opened my mouth to warn her, but what could I say? Only Mrs. Nasser took her outstretched hand. Mr. Nasser smiled and bowed his head, avoiding Mrs. Marino's eyes. Mrs. Marino realized, too late, her error and let her hand fall to her side; it wasn't proper for a Muslim man to shake hands with a woman.

"Amira will be here for half a day, just to get acquainted with the school. Will you bring her back to the office at lunchtime? Her parents will come to pick her up." I nodded, relieved I wouldn't have to miss basketball tryouts to play tour guide. I waved goodbye to the Nassers as Amira and I walked into the hallway.

The halls were quiet, and so was Amira. I led her toward the gym, the first place I'd wanted to see when I arrived in Canada. In Syria, we'd had gym classes outside on the cracked pavement of the school courtyard. I hadn't understood why gym class was held indoors until my first winter. Then it all made sense! "Where are you from?" I asked in Arabic. She looked at me like I'd asked a trick question. "I grew up in Damascus," I told her, "in Mezzah." It was a neighbourhood with cafés and stores and an outdoor shopping centre. Lots of doctors and lawyers lived in our building.

"We are from Homs." Her voice was quiet, a little raspy.

I knew of Homs. I'd seen it on the news. There was almost nothing left of it. My insides churned for her. I wanted to ask how long she'd been away from Syria. Her journey to Canada wouldn't have been like mine. Staying with family in Yorkshire had been like a reunion while we waited for our immigration papers to Canada. We'd arrived in Toronto and come straight to Winnipeg so Dad could start his job. The university found us temporary housing while we looked for a house to buy; containers with our things waited in storage for us. We'd left before the refugee crisis, not like Amira, who had been forced to flee. There had been no choice for her family. If we'd stayed longer, we might have been like them.

"This is the gym," I said, pausing at the door. Kids ran past, doing laps for warm-up. Amira hung back, reluctant to get closer. She took in the size of the gym, with its shiny wooden floors and huge Thunder logo painted on the cinder-block walls. I got an anxious twinge thinking about what tomorrow would be like for her: showing up for a full day of school with no idea what awaited. She'd need to stick close to me or she wouldn't find her way around. For the next few weeks, Amira was going to be attached to me. I hoped it was just first-day jitters that kept her so quiet, otherwise it was going to be a long term.

"Come on, I'll show you the cafeteria." We went downstairs to the row of picnic-style tables. I walked through the space quickly, trying to get the tour over with so we could get to class. "This is where you'll eat lunch, when you stay for lunch. Microwaves are over there." I pointed to the far wall. "And the canteen. They sell fries, burgers, hot dogs, Pizza Pops, stuff like that."

"Pizza Pops?"

"Like a pizza sandwich," I explained.

She furrowed her brow. Without any students, the cafeteria felt cavernous. Our voices echoed.

"Do you pray?" she asked. In Syria, prayers were a normal part of the day; classes were scheduled around prayer times. In Canada, fitting in midday prayers at school was a little trickier.

"There's a room we use. I can show it to you now, if you want."

Amira nodded, so we went back upstairs. "It's here," I said, pointing to a room with desks and a few computers in it. There was construction paper over the small window on the door to give us privacy and a movable screen to separate the male and female sides of the room.

The truth was, Mariam and I had barely used the room set aside for our prayers this year. Now that I was in high school, I was self-conscious about disappearing at lunchtime. And since basketball tryouts had started, I knew it was even more unlikely that I'd pray at midday like I was supposed to.

"Are there lots of Muslim students?" Amira asked.

"Not that many. In our homeroom there's me, Mariam, and Mohammed, and now you."

I pointed out the washrooms she would use as we walked back to Mr. Letner's room. "Everyone here is really nice. You'll like it here."

"How long have you been here? In Canada?" she asked.

"About three years — almost four. We were in the U.K. for a while before we got here."

"Is your English good?"

It was *now*. "My dad spoke it at home sometimes in Syria to get us ready, but mostly I just learned by living here."

"You knew you were leaving."

"Sort of. We knew we were going somewhere."

"Some of our family is in Germany, but they'd closed the borders by the time we left. This was the only country that would take us."

"My family is in England. Aunts, cousins, my sitta. We all left before things got bad."

She snorted. "You don't know bad."

I gave her a sideways look and wondered what she meant. What had she seen in Syria or the camps they'd lived in? For someone who was the same age as me, she seemed so much older. I could only imagine that what she'd lived through had aged her. I felt a flash of gratitude that I wasn't like her. Making the co-ed team was my biggest worry. "This is our class." I pointed to Mr. Letner's nameplate above the door and the room number, 9B. "I'll quickly introduce you and you can sit down. Don't worry if you can't understand anything."

I hadn't known what was going on for the first few weeks, either. I'd just followed the other kids, watching what they were doing, too scared to ask any questions. At recess, things felt more normal. I learned the kids' names on the soccer field, and when we played games in class, I could figure out the rules and participate. But as soon as the teacher started talking, or we had to get a book to read, I drifted off and missed my school in Syria where everything made sense and where asking a simple question like "Can I go to the washroom?" wasn't a stressful situation. I'd been a good student in Syria, but in Canada the language barrier had made it hard to prove. Dad had warned us it would be like trying to ride a bicycle with your feet tied together: you knew how, but couldn't make it happen. *And* it was very frustrating.

"Okay, ready?" I asked her, but I'd already opened the door to the class. Mr. Letner turned to me.

"Is this our new student?"

I nodded. "Her name is Amira. She doesn't speak English," I blurted out for her.

"Thanks, Sadia," Mr. Letner said. "Amira, you can sit there." He spoke slowly and pointed to a chair he'd already moved to my table. There wasn't really space for her, so Carmina and Mariam squished together. I led the way and tried to give her an encouraging smile, even though inside, I groaned. I'd have to spend the morning translating instead of doing my own work, which would mean more homework tonight.

Amira sat down at the desk and stared at her hands. I dug through my backpack for a pen and took a piece of loose-leaf out of my binder and put it in front of her. I had no idea what she would write on it.

"Where's she from?" Mariam scribbled on my page.

"Syria," I wrote back.

She leaned forward and tried to catch Amira's eye. "Hi!" she whispered. Either Amira didn't hear, or she ignored her, but either way, Mariam shrugged and sat back in her chair, as if she'd done all she could.

When the bell rang for second period, I jumped up and packed my binder into my backpack. "What about the new girl?" Carmina reminded me as we filed out with the rest of the class. I looked back. Amira was standing beside the desk, looking lost.

"Right," I mumbled under my breath. I forgot I was babysitting today. And then I felt bad for thinking like that. I'd had to rely on the kindness of others when we'd first moved here, just like Amira was relying on me now.

"It's gym," I told her in Arabic. She looked at me with panicked eyes. "Don't worry, you can probably just sit and watch the class on your first day."

"Boys and girls have gym together?" she asked in a rushed whisper.

"Yes." I'd forgotten how different things would be for her here. I'd been eleven when we'd moved, still a kid compared to Amira. Things like co-ed gym classes hadn't been any different from home.

I explained to Mr. McMurchy, the gym teacher, that Amira was new and didn't speak much English. "I think she just wants to sit out and watch," I told him.

"Okay, but only for today, since it's her first day." I translated for Amira, and the briefest of relieved smiles crossed her face. I didn't translate the second half of his answer: "Next time, she joins in."

Grateful to have a break from being her translator and tour guide, I went to change into my gym clothes. When I came out, Josh had already started running laps so I joined him, our steps in rhythm as we talked about which kids had the best shot of making the team. I had to run faster than usual to keep up with him and could feel my heart pumping. As a few more of his friends started running, we got separated and I ran at the front of a clump of girls. I almost stumbled over my shoes when I looked at the change room doors and saw Mariam in shorts and a gym shirt. She must have borrowed them from Carmina. She stood there self-consciously, starting an awkward run-walk on the periphery of the track.

I slowed my pace to join her, gaping at her bare legs. "Mariam!" I hissed. "What are you doing?"

"It's just gym clothes. We used to change all the time." *When we were kids!* I thought. Her parents would be furious if they saw her. I didn't know what to say to her, so I sprinted ahead, my hijab flapping behind me.

CHAPTER 5

"You're not going to tell anyone, are you?" Mariam asked in Arabic as we walked back to class after gym.

"No," I answered, kind of mad that she even had to ask. "But you know it's wrong," I whispered.

Mariam gave me a pleading look. "Please don't say anything."

"I won't," I promised. I wasn't her parent. It wasn't up to me to force modesty on her, but I couldn't help feeling that her decisions were putting more and more distance between us. I liked that we both wore hijab; it was our thing — it separated us from all the other girls in our class. If she kept changing (and I didn't just mean her clothes), what would happen to us?

And if I did tell on her, it would be a betrayal of our friendship, which would only drive her further away. She'd pushed me into an impossible corner.

"Promise?" she asked again. I gave her a solemn nod. As soon as she was satisfied that I'd keep her secret, she drifted away from me and found Carmina. The two of them walked to their next class together. From the excited chatter, I guessed that Mariam was telling

Carmina how good it had felt to wear shorts again. I watched them jealously for a minute and pulled my eyes away. It used to be Mariam and *me* who were close.

Amira followed me like a shadow to my locker as I grabbed a snack, stuffed my gym bag in, and got my books for the rest of the morning.

"Your friend Mariam," Amira asked quietly. "Is she Muslim?"

"Yeah. She's from Egypt."

"But she doesn't wear hijab."

"Usually she does." I wished I could have explained more, but Mariam's behaviour was becoming a mystery to me.

"Okay, everyone. Sit down. Break's over." Mr. Letner stood at the front of the room with the suitcase of digital cameras. "I've heard back from almost everyone's parents, giving permission to let you take the cameras home. Those of you whose parents haven't emailed the form back can take pictures today, you just can't take the cameras home." He held up his hands, as if quieting an unruly crowd. "I know, I know. You're thinking, 'Mr. Letner, I already know how to use a camera. I've been taking pictures on my iPad since I was little.' But just snapping a photo and taking a picture of something that captures the imagination of the viewer are two different things." He slowed his voice down, so we'd all pay attention. "For example, as a famous Russian writer once said, 'Don't tell me the moon is shining; show me the glint of light on broken glass.'"

I looked over at Amira. The blank look on her face told me she had no idea what he was talking about.

Mr. Letner turned off the front row of lights, and immediately a bunch of kids put their heads on their desks, ready to zone out. An image appeared on the Smartboard. "Even ordinary things can become powerful images. Look at this one." A fingerprint: the black ink on the stark white page filled up the screen. Mr. Letner scanned the room. "What do you think about it? What's your reaction?"

"It's a fingerprint," Avery said, unimpressed. "We all have them."

"Do you?"

"Yeah, I mean they're not all the same, but —" And then she caught herself. "Oh, I get it. The photo is showing how we're all different."

Mr. Letner touched his nose and pointed at Avery. "There you go! One image, but lots of meanings. Here, look at this one." Another photo appeared, and at first, I didn't know what it was. A round ball with bubbles suspended in its centre. The glass glowed like something from another world, the swirl inside of it like a tornado. It was a marble sitting on concrete. The pebbled surface was rough and pitted against the smoothness of the glass. "Pretty cool, eh?" I leaned forward in my seat, waiting for the next image.

"Do you know what this is?" It was a photo of a snowbank half-melted into the shape of an elephant. We all laughed. Well, not Amira. She was probably like me before my first Canadian winter, when I'd never touched snow.

"The next photo I'm going to show you is shocking," he warned us. The image of a starving African child crouched on the ground appeared on the screen. She was skin and bones, every rib visible. In the background, a vulture waited. "Is that for real?" Zander asked.

Mr. Letner nodded. "This photo was taken during the Sudanese famine. It made international news and won the Pulitzer Prize."

"I hope whoever took the photo helped her, gave her food or something," Carmina muttered, and looked away.

"This photo showed the world what was going on in the Sudan. Up until then, no one had paid much attention to the famine. I want you to really think about what you photograph. Use your photos to show people how you see the world, or to help change it. It might mean looking at the world differently or seeing details in things you wouldn't normally notice, like a marble, or a snowbank. Or making a social commentary on a problem that bothers you."

I was relieved when the photo of the starving child disappeared. "Do you expect our photos to look like those ones?" Larissa asked. "They're, like, *professional*."

"It's the idea behind the photo I want you to think about. The technique will come with practise. We'll start today by playing around with the cameras and taking some pictures."

Mr. Letner passed out the cameras and wrote down which number each of us had.

Amira fingered the camera in front of her like it was something suspicious. "This is a camera," I said slowly in English.

"This is a camera," she repeated quietly.

Beside me, Carmina and Mariam snapped pouty-lipped pictures of each other, the standard selfie pose. Even though Mr. Letner had said not to take selfies, they couldn't help themselves. When I looked around the room, a lot of other people were doing the same thing. "Can you get one of both of us?" Carmina asked me, holding her camera out.

I hesitated. Did Mariam realize how excluded I felt watching the two of them? "And then take one of me and Sadia," Mariam said to Carmina.

They turned their chins down and gave a coy look to the camera. Then I gave my camera to Carmina, and Mariam and I huddled together. But before she took the photo, I held up my hand. "Wait." Amira was on my other side. "Come on, you should be in the picture, too. It's your first day at a Canadian school," I said to her in Arabic. I held out my arm for her to slide closer. She looked like she was about to shake her head, but then she relented and joined us. Carmina took the photo and passed the camera back to me. I looked at the image. Mariam and I were grinning, but Amira just stared into the camera, her eyes open, wide and wary.

CHAPTER 6

I walked Amira back to the office to meet her parents when the lunch bell rang. She held the camera in her hands like it was a treasure. She hadn't taken any photos yet; it was almost like she was worried she'd break it. "How did it go?" Mrs. Mooney asked as we sat waiting for Amira's parents in the office. I turned to Amira, who gave Mrs. Mooney a shy smile. "Sadia, can you translate this list of school supplies for Amira's parents? And there's the media release letter." She rattled off all the other information I'd have to explain. So much for lunch. It was going to take me half an hour to go over all this with them.

There was a bustle in the office entrance as Mr. and Mrs. Nasser walked in. They greeted their daughter and me with anxious smiles. They had lots of questions for Amira, but she looked exhausted and waved them off. I remembered what those first weeks had been like. Trying to make sense of what everyone was saying was tiring! My brain hurt when I got home after school, new words and images swirling through my head. And when it was time to go to sleep, my brain was so jumbled with English and Arabic words that I couldn't turn it off. "The school needs you to sign some things," I told Amira's parents. I showed them all the papers, doing my best to explain what they meant. There was also a paper copy of the permission form from Mr. Letner. He'd asked me to translate it for them and have them sign it for him. Mr. Nasser gave me a puzzled look as I'd explained the project, but scribbled his signature anyway. Dad used to question some of the activities the school planned when we first moved here, too. He'd gone along with them, though, just like Mr. Nasser did, but there was a big difference between how schools were run in Syria and in Canada.

Amira didn't say goodbye as she left the office. She bowed her head and shuffled behind her parents, even when her mom took her hand and tried to pry some information out of her. I knew how she felt. It was like a tidal wave of information had just splashed over her, and she'd only been at school for a few hours. She could never explain it all to her mother. I glanced at the clock. Basketball tryouts started in five minutes. I'd have to run to the cafeteria, scarf down my lunch, and then head to the gym with food sloshing in my stomach.

I don't think Mr. Letner knew what a stir he was going to cause when he gave us those cameras. Kids from other classes kept posing in the hallway, begging us to take their pictures. And before basketball club, no one wanted to practise. Instead, we asked Jillian to do jump shots so we could practise taking action shots.

"Will you take one of me?" I asked Josh, handing him my camera. I held the basketball against my hip and smiled. He held the camera up to his eye for a second but didn't take the picture.

"Nah, it's all wrong," he said, shaking his head.

"What is?" I asked, confused.

He nodded to the wall behind me. "It would look better if you were at the top of the key with the hoop behind you." Josh walked over to me and pulled me by my elbow into a better position. Then he took the basketball and bent my arm so it was balanced on my palm.

"I feel like one of those fake people in a store window," I said, rolling my eyes.

"A mannequin," he said. "Yeah, except mannequins don't have killer crossovers."

His compliment made me blush. My crossovers weren't *that* good.

He took three giant steps backward. It was only as I smiled into the camera that I saw Mariam staring at me from behind Josh, her eyes narrowed. I stood awkwardly as Josh played around with the settings and circled me, trying to get just the right angle and lighting. Mariam glared at me and went off in a huff.

"Oh, great," I muttered.

"Cameras away!" Mr. Letner shouted. "They shouldn't be out during basketball practice." He picked up his clipboard. "Same deal as last time. Drills and then a scrimmage." This time, I made sure my hijab was on securely so I wouldn't get any more bloody noses. I held my own when we scrimmaged, and the bell for the end of lunch came too soon. There was a stampede for the change rooms, but I had an idea for a photo and hung back.

"Josh," I said. "Can you help me with something? I want to take a photo of a ball being tossed into the bin."

He gave me a funny look but agreed. "Yeah, sure."

He stood a few metres back, far enough that he wasn't in the shot, and tossed the ball in an arc toward the bin. It landed, jostling the others so they bounced. I snapped a few shots in a row of the ball moving through the air and then landing in the bin, jostling the others. "Cool," I said, reviewing them. "Thanks!"

"No problem."

Allan came out of the boys' change room just as I was about to go into the girls'. "Hey, man, what are you doing?" I heard him ask Josh.

"Taking some pictures with Sadia," Josh answered.

"Sadia?" Allan mocked. "Why are you wasting your time with *her*? Dude, Jillian Triggs was here. That's who I'd be taking pictures of." I could imagine him moving his eyebrows up and down suggestively.

Josh snorted and didn't say anything for a minute. "Yeah, I know, right?"

I froze for a second, my throat tightening at their words. I let the door shut silently behind me, grateful that the other girls were too intent on getting changed to question the scowl on my face. Allan's scornful tone echoed in my head. A waste of time? Was that what Josh really thought of me?

"How was basketball?" Mariam asked when I sat down beside her for English. I wasn't in the mood for her snarky tone. Did she really want to know, or did she just want to accuse me of flirting with Josh? The same Josh who had just "wasted his time" with me. I tried to ignore her, but she asked again.

"It was fine," I said curtly and hoped she'd drop it.

"Are you hiding something?" She grabbed my camera out of my hands and started going through my photos.

"Hey!" I said and reached for it, but she twisted further away.

"What? Something on here you don't want me to see?"

"No," I said, indignant. I refused to sink to the level of fighting her for my camera, so I let her click through the photos. She wasn't going to find anything incriminating, anyway. Josh walked into the class, his hair spiked with sweat, and her demeanour instantly changed.

"Great shot of Sadia," Mariam said to him.

Josh looked confused until she held up the camera to show him. He glanced at me, but I looked away. *Jerk.*

"Thanks," Josh said and made a hasty retreat to the back of the room.

"Why are you being like this?" I hissed at her. "Fighting with me over a guy? He's not worth it, by the way."

Mariam glared at me and looked like she wanted to say something else, but didn't.

For the rest of the afternoon, Mariam and I sat in a prickly silence, both of us too stubborn to talk. And at the end of the day, when Josh walked past my locker and said, "See you," I ignored him. I didn't bother to wait for Mariam at the end of the day either. I knew she wouldn't take the bus with me, and I'd taken as much rejection for one day as I could handle.

CHAPTER 7

I flashed my bus pass to the driver and walked down the aisle to find a seat. A large woman, propping up her top half with a cane, flicked a glance at my hijab, her wrinkly jowls dangling at her chin. Her small eyes folded into her flesh as her offhand glance turned into a suspicious stare. A little voice told me to stare back at her, but I knew that would be rude. *She's being rude,* the voice responded. I tried to silence the voice, like Mom would do. She'd hold her head high and walk past, classy and aloof, passing off the woman's stare as curiosity, when we both knew it was more than that.

I glanced once at the lady as I sat down, my own curiosity getting the best of me. Maybe it would be better to stand right in front of her, let her stare all she wanted, and talk to her. Maybe if she got to know me, she'd see I'm normal … well, as normal as anyone else. Including her.

Wearing hijab set me apart from other people on the bus; it announced who I was before anything else. People see my hijab and know I'm Muslim. And *I'm* cool with that, but it was obvious from the way

this lady was staring at me that she wasn't. It made a
scream rise up in my throat. *You don't even know me!*
I wanted to yell at her. *Stop staring!* I looked out the
window beside me as buildings slipped by, praying that
the woman would get off at the next stop. But it was
me who got off before her. I felt my cheeks get hot as
I walked past her, angry that I had to deal with her
looks, on top of everything else.

Mom knew something was wrong as soon as I
walked into the kitchen after school. Telling her about
the lady on the bus was pointless; there was nothing she
could do about it. Part of me wanted to tell her about
my argument with Mariam, but I'd sworn I wouldn't tell
anyone about her now daily de-jabbing. So instead, I
dumped my backpack on the floor and groaned.

"Sadia?" Mom looked at me, puzzled. She was getting dinner started in the kitchen, chopping vegetables
on the wooden cutting board. "What's wrong?"

"I just have a lot of homework." I sighed. There was
a new stack of library books on the counter, which was
normal; Mom went to the library all the time, but something about these ones caught my eye.

"Are those books in Arabic?"

Mom nodded. "Remember, I told you about the
new Arabic section at the library? I took the bus downtown to check it out."

"Cool."

"I had a long talk with the head librarian." Mom
raised an eyebrow secretively.

I turned to her, giving her my full attention.
"Really?"

"I'm going to start volunteering there." She looked up from the cutting board. "They don't have anyone on site who speaks Arabic."

"Mom! That's great!"

She waved a hand at me, like I shouldn't get too excited. "I worry about my English …" She let her words drift off.

"It's getting better every day," I said, switching from Arabic to English. "You just need to keep practising, speak English to us instead of Arabic." I pulled my homework out of my backpack. Hearing Mom's good news took some of the sting out of my day. "A new girl started today. Amira Nasser."

"Where's she from?"

"Homs."

"Syria? She's a refugee?"

"I think so."

Mom's face fell, her eyebrows knitted together. "Do you know anything else? Where they're living? How many people are in their family?" The Syrian population in our city was small, but close-knit. The refugees had added a new dimension to our group of family friends. Conversation at family functions had turned away from politics and the war to what would happen to the refugees. I shook my head no to answer her questions. "Find out, will you? We can invite them over."

Mom looked up from making dinner as I pulled the camera, tucked inside its black nylon case, out of my backpack.

"Is that the camera?" she asked.

"Yeah. I already took some photos at school."

"Let me guess, basketball?"

I nodded. "I wish it was warmer out so I could take some of Aazim playing in the driveway."

"Take one of Aazim studying. That's where his energy needs to be now."

I rolled my eyes. Mom was so predictable. Education was the number-one most important thing to my parents. Once they'd decided Aazim was going to be a doctor, Dad had determined I'd be an engineer. If he'd asked me, I'd have told him I wanted to be the next Kia Nurse and play basketball for Team Canada.

"Can I see?" she asked, coming around the counter. She had it out of the pouch before I could say no.

"Here, let me show you," I said and took it from her before she could turn it on. The first photo was one of Mariam *without her head scarf*. I held it close to my chest and clicked past the incriminating shot, then passed it to her.

She grinned as I showed her pictures of basketball tryouts and the one of me that Josh had taken. She pressed the arrow button for the next picture, but instead of stopping like my iPhone did, it went back to the beginning. "Is that Mariam?" she asked, leaning closer to the camera. The three of us — me, Amira, and Mariam — looked back from the screen. Two with head scarves, one without.

Mom's eyebrows shot up. I turned the camera off quickly. *Oh boy.*

"Why isn't she in hijab?"

"Don't say anything to her parents, okay? She'll never speak to me again."

"They should know."

"Not from us."

Mom pursed her lips. "Do you do that? Change at school?"

I shook my head. "No, never." She gave me a searching look, as if she could tell if I was being dishonest. "Really, Mom. I wouldn't do that." She looked like she wanted to give me a speech about the tenets of Islam and why modesty was important, why wearing hijab mattered.

"I hope not," was all she said. She went back to chopping onions and I looked at the photo again. I should delete the photo. Erasing the evidence would be what a good friend would do, but her snarky attitude had left a bad taste in my mouth. I kept the photo.

CHAPTER 8

"Hi, Amira," I greeted her. She was waiting in the office for me, sitting across from Mrs. Mooney's desk, holding a backpack on her lap. When she saw me, she stood up.

"Hi," she said in English. "How are you?" Her accent was strong, but I gave her a big grin of encouragement. I remembered how scary it was to try out those first words.

"I'm good. How are you?"

She nodded. "Fine." After that, we stood looking at each other because neither of us knew what else to say in English or Arabic.

"We can go to class," I suggested. "Mr. Letner will let us in. He arrives early." Amira followed me down the hallway. "Did you take photos?" I asked her, holding up my camera.

"Yes. A lot. I wish I could send the photos to the camps, so they could see what it is like here."

I turned to her. I'd seen the camps on TV. Syrians who had left their homes but hadn't made it across to Europe lived in settlements in Lebanon. The tents and lean-tos stretched for kilometres and the refugees lived like homeless people. Not *like* homeless people, they *were* homeless. They'd given up their homes to flee the war. Despite that, the refugees had created a life in the camps, complete with makeshift schools, restaurants, and shops. "That's where you were?"

"For almost a year."

I imagined what this school, with its clean, orderly desks and healthy, well-fed students, must feel like for her. "Then we were in a hotel for a month, waiting for a place to live in Winnipeg."

"How many people are in your family?"

"Seven. I am the oldest. I have four younger brothers."

I looked at her, incredulous. "*Four* little brothers." It would be her responsibility to look after them.

"Who watched them when your parents came with you yesterday? Or were they at school?"

"The littlest one is only two, but Omar, Sami, and Yussef start school next week, so a worker came over. She comes to visit us, teaches us to do things, shows us things. She's bringing a TV today. I can't wait." It was the first time I saw a flicker of life cross her face.

"Can I see your photos?" I asked. She gave me a wary look, like a skittish cat. "Here, I'll show you mine," I offered.

I'd taken a lot around the house yesterday. Close-ups of my family, including one of my dad snoring in a chair as he slept through the news, my room, and the prayer mat in the dining room with the early evening sun streaming through. The last picture was of my basketball shoes, dirty and crumpled, with the laces hanging limp, as if they were exhausted from overuse. I smiled as I showed it to her. "That's my favourite."

"You are a big fan of basketball?"

"Yes! What about you? Do you play?" The haunted look she had when I'd met her yesterday returned. She shook her head.

"In Homs, the army planted bombs around the playground."

"Oh." The smile on my face disappeared. I'd left years before her, but it may as well have been a lifetime. The Syria I remembered was nothing like the one she'd been living in.

"Hi, girls." Mr. Letner motioned for us to come inside the class. "Amira," he gave her an extra-big smile, but she ducked and sat down in the chair beside my spot. I shrugged at Mr. Letner as if to say, *What can we do?* and sat down.

Mr. Letner had booked lab time so we could download and edit our photos. I'd already decided that no matter how Mariam acted toward me, I'd pretend things were fine between us. Maybe her rude behaviour was a phase and she'd be back to the old Mariam soon.

But not soon enough. She walked in again without hijab, wearing another one of Carmina's shirts, one of those long-sleeved, close-fitting athletic ones that I sometimes wore under a looser shirt. She'd put her hair up in a ponytail and was wearing stretchy, black pants and tall, black boots. I had to admit, the outfit looked good on her, and it looked comfortable. For a second, I wondered how it would feel to play basketball wearing an outfit like that — well maybe not with the boots....

Mariam sat down and didn't say hello to me or Amira. Her icy silence tempted me to wave my hands in her face and act like an idiot just to annoy her. Instead, I concentrated on helping Amira by pointing at things in the classroom and saying the English word. Mr. Letner gave me a thumbs-up. Josh walked in just before the bell. I carefully avoided his gaze. The more I'd thought about Allan's comment, the more I wondered what Josh really thought about me. He could have stuck up for me and told Allan that we were friends, but he hadn't. I think I was more hurt by his betrayal than by what Allan had said.

Carmina and Mariam kept writing notes to each other and passing them under the desk. I tried to ignore them, but I couldn't help wondering if they were about me. Every time they stifled a giggle, I sat up straighter, focusing on Mr. Letner, or helping Amira make sense of what he was saying. I was determined not to let Mariam get to me.

"Now that you've all got some photos, we can go to the computer lab and start playing around with effects using Photoshop." He took a photo he'd taken of trees in a field and demonstrated. First, he changed the whole photo to black and white. Next, he showed us how to crop the photo so only the most important things were included, like the trees. Then, he zoomed in and enlarged the trees so they took up the whole frame. He brightened the sky and darkened one tree so it stood out against the grass. By the time he was done, the photo was a piece of art.

"Select the photos you want to upload, then play around with them. When you have one you want to share, save it in our shared student drive and you can present it to the class."

The computer lab was noisy as everyone showed each other their photos. I worked quietly, sorting and editing my pictures but it was hard not to peer over Amira's shoulder to see what she was working on. Mr. Letner walked around, helping kids who needed it. Despite my feelings toward Josh, I'd chosen the photo he had taken of me holding the basketball. I knew it would annoy Mariam to see it on the Smartboard screen, but I didn't care. It was my favourite one. I liked that it made me look strong. Not your stereotypical Muslim girl, that's for sure. Plus, the grin on my face stretched ear to ear. I changed it to black and white, cropped the background, and enlarged the image so the basketball was in the centre of the frame. From across the lab, Carmina and Mariam were oohing over each other's photos. Mariam and I should be doing that, I thought. Why weren't we? Was it just because of the hijab? Or Josh? Or maybe, and this part was hard to think about, we really were growing apart....

"Sadia?" Amira turned her screen so I could see her photo. "Can you help me?" she asked in Arabic.

I realized she didn't know what any of the English words meant on the screen, so for the last thirty minutes, she'd been randomly moving the mouse around, trying to make something happen. I translated the words and showed her what each icon did.

Mr. Letner came around again and congratulated me on my photo. "Save it to the shared drive. I'll show it to everyone when we're back in the classroom."

I thought again of Mariam and what she'd say when my smiling face came up on the screen. She'd know it was the photo Josh had taken of me. Did I really want to make things worse between us? "No," I said, shaking my head. I'd changed my mind. "I don't want to share it."

Mr. Letner frowned. "Really? You did a great job on it."

I shook my head again. He sighed. "Okay."

On Amira's screen was a new photo. She'd taken it at a grocery store. In her hand was an orange, and behind the one she was holding, a pyramid of a hundred more. "Orange," I said, without thinking.

"Yummy," she said in perfect English.

I smiled at her.

She continued in Arabic: "We had an orange tree in our yard. I used to pick them to eat for breakfast." We'd had a fig tree on our balcony in Syria. There was no better treat than a sun-warmed fig melting on my tongue. It had been years since I'd had one, but the taste and feel of them flooded back to me.

"The tree is dead now," she said with finality. I looked at her, alarmed. But there was no emotion on her face. Was it dead because no one was there to look after it, or for another reason?

"Amira," I started, prepared to say something to let her know I understood how hard moving to a new country was: the homesickness and feeling like she didn't belong. But as I opened my mouth, Mr. Letner drew our attention back to him.

"Okay, everyone. Save your work and log off. We'll continue this tomorrow. Remember, keep taking pictures. I really like what I've seen so far."

I showed Amira how to save her photos. I took an extra-long time to make sure that Mariam and Carmina had left the lab before I stood up to leave. "Lunch?" Amira asked in English.

"You're staying?"

She nodded.

"I have basketball tryouts," I told her. "You can come."

She shook her head and looked at the floor. "No, I don't think so."

"Why not?"

Amira shrugged. "I don't know the game."

If she'd said she hated basketball, I would have let it go. You can't force someone to love a sport. But not knowing how to play? That part, I could fix.

CHAPTER 9

The pimpled rubber of the basketball lay under my fingers. I bounced it once. Hand, floor, hand. "See?" I showed Amira. "Easy."

She dropped her ball and caught it. "Easy."

I dropped my ball, dribbled it twice, and caught it. Amira dropped her ball, but she held her hand too flat and got no bounce. It rolled into her toe. She grimaced at me. "Try again," I told her. This time, I showed her how to push her hand against the ball so it would rebound off the floor. She had to chase it to keep the dribble going, but she got six bounces in a row before she lost it.

"Okay, now, a bounce pass." She put her ball down. I sent my ball to her with a gentle bounce. She caught it and grinned at me. "Nice!" We went back and forth like that for a while. "Try this: dribble, dribble, dribble, bounce pass." The first two tries were fails, but the third one she did perfectly. As kids started to arrive for the tryouts, I thought Amira would be too embarrassed to keep playing, but I was wrong. It made me wonder if the shy girl who'd arrived at school was the real Amira.

"Hey," Josh called, walking over. Startled by his voice, Amira missed the pass and the ball bounced past her. I ignored him and waited for Amira to get the ball. "Sadia?" he said tentatively.

"What?"

"Are you okay?"

I set my mouth and refused to look at him.

"Cuz I thought we could practise our free throws —"

Mariam walked over to us from the gym doorway. "Is it three throws or free throws?" She knew the right term, and it made me grit my teeth hearing her act dumb to get Josh's attention.

"*Free* throw," Josh said.

"Oh," she said as if he'd just explained nuclear fission to her. For the first time, she noticed Amira standing beside me. "Is she trying out, too?" she asked incredulously.

I didn't bother to answer and rolled my eyes at Mariam. She could have asked Amira herself in Arabic.

It was almost time for tryouts to begin, so I explained to Amira that she could wait on the bench for me while I went to get changed. I was relieved to walk away from both Josh and Mariam, although I did wonder why Josh had asked to practise his free throws with me instead of Jillian.

When I came out of the change room, Amira was sitting on the bench and Mariam was talking with Mr. Letner. She had her all-business face on, which meant she was determined and wouldn't take no for an answer. She'd convinced my parents into many sleepovers using that face. I wondered what she wanted from Mr. Letner.

I adjusted my hijab and ran onto the court. Jillian did a layup and the ball rebounded off the backboard and straight into her hands. She took another shot: it rolled around the rim and down, but I was underneath the basket and lunged for it. I caught the ball and felt it slap against my palm. I took a breath and aimed. The ball sailed in. I could lose myself in playing, the squeak of runners on the shellacked floor and the echo of the ball against the cement walls. Even the smell of rubber was comforting. While I played, I could forget about Josh and that my *supposed* best friend was turning into someone I didn't know. Someone I didn't even want to know.

Mr. Letner had promised us that he'd announce who was making the team by the end of the next day. I got butterflies thinking about it. We'd have a few weeks to practise before the tournament. It would mean giving up lunch hours and maybe some early mornings. "Good practice," he said to me as we walked back to the classroom. "I noticed Amira was watching. Does she play?"

"She's just learning," I told him.

"I really like how you've taken her under your wing, Sadia. Thanks."

I shrugged off his compliment, but it made me feel good to know that at least he'd noticed.

"I thought Mariam might help out, too."

I tried to keep my expression the same at the mention of her name.

"I noticed she's not wearing her head scarf anymore." He gave me a long look before we turned into the hallway.

All the things I wanted to say bubbled up in my throat. "She still does around her parents," I said. "Just not at school."

"How's that sit with you?"

I shrugged. What could I say? That I hated it and wanted to duct tape the hijab back on her head? "If her parents found out, they'd be really mad."

"Sounds like you're in a tough spot."

I waited for Mr. Letner to give me some brilliant wisdom, but all he did was gently slap my shoulder and tell me to hurry up and get my books or I'd be late for class.

I was at my locker when I heard "Sadia!" from down the hallway. It was Josh, but I ignored him and quickly stashed my gym bag and basketball shoes. I wasn't fast enough, though, and when I shut the locker door, Josh was on the other side of it.

He ran a hand through his damp hair, pushing it off his forehead. "Did I do something to piss you off?" he asked.

Being honest about what I'd overheard would have been the smart thing to do, but the hurt I'd felt when he agreed with Allan made being smart impossible. Anger at Mariam and her stupid de-jabbing bubbled up, too, and before I could stop myself, words spewed out of my mouth like a verbal volcano. "Mariam likes you," I blurted. "I know she's no Jillian Triggs, but hopefully she's not a waste of time like I am." I turned on my heel to walk away before he could see the blush spreading across my face.

"Who said you're a waste of time? And what's Jillian got to do with anything?" he called after me. My plan was to march away from him, breeze into class, and pretend like nothing had happened. Of course, that didn't go as planned, either.

"Whoa!" Josh said, grabbing my arm. "What's going on? You *are* mad at me!"

"No, I'm not." I shook my arm out of his grip, but I could feel my cheeks burning.

He gave me a doubtful look. I stared back, keeping my gaze level. "Really? Cuz when you make the team, we'll have to play together for the next month."

I rolled my eyes. "You don't know I'm going to make the team."

During tryouts, I'd scoped out the other girls and gotten nervous. Jillian was the most talented, but a few other girls, like Jeein and Sarah, had surprised me with their skills. Mr. Letner only had to choose four of us. What if I didn't make the cut?

"Yeah, I do. You're one of the best girls out there. Anyhow, I wouldn't want to play on a team that you weren't on."

His words caught me off guard and I paused, confused.

Mr. Letner poked his head out of the classroom, scanning the hallway for latecomers. "Come on, you two, hurry up," he called. I let Josh walk in the room a few steps ahead of me. Even though my body was in the classroom, my mind was in the hallway. What did Josh mean when he said he wouldn't play on a team without me? What about his conversation with Allan?

I sighed as I sat down and ignored Mariam's questioning stare.

CHAPTER 10

"As promised," Mr. Letner said when everyone was seated the next day for first period Global Issues, "we'll start with your photos. Who wants to go first? Zander?"

Zander stood up and looked out at everyone. I knew why Mr. Letner had picked him to go first. He loved being the centre of attention. I sat back, ready to be entertained. "Okay, so for my photo, I wanted to show something that has a lot of meaning to me. I have this stuffie —" The class burst into laughter. Zander laughed, too. "I don't sleep with him anymore," he said quickly, "but I wanted to take a picture of him cuz he means a lot to me." Mr. Letner clicked on the photo from his computer and a close-up shot of a brown-and-white spotted stuffed dog came on the screen. The way Zander had posed him, it looked like his stuffie was staring out the window on the back of a couch, the way real dogs sometimes do. Zander sounded a little more nervous as he watched us looking at his photo. "Mr. Letner said ordinary things have meaning. So I took this picture of Whiffer, my stuffie, because when I was a kid, I used to leave him sitting on the back of the couch when I went to school so that when I came home, I'd see him waiting for me."

Carmina made a face at Mariam and me, as if Zander was the cutest guy ever. It *was* impressive that he'd had the guts to go first and to show a photo of a stuffed animal.

"Awww. That is *soooo* cute, Zander," Allan said mockingly from the back of the room.

Mr. Letner silenced him with a look and turned his attention to Zander. "How does it show perspective?"

"When I was a kid, Whiffer was super important, but now that I'm older …" Zander let his words trail off.

"Your priorities have changed."

"Which is kind of like my perspective has changed."

"Thanks, Zander. Takes a big man to admit he sleeps with stuffies."

"*Used* to sleep with stuffies," Zander corrected him and went back to his seat.

"But he's not just a stuffie, is he?" Mr. Letner continued. "Your dog represents childhood and all the things that come with having a toy you love. I'm sure lots of you have toys that are special to you. Or were special to you when you were a kid. Might be a good topic for some more photos. I bet a lot of you have your favourite toy stuffed in your closet. Am I right? You don't need it anymore, but you don't want to let it go, either. That perspective on growing up would make a good photo."

I thought about Bibi. I'd had her since I was born, a rabbit with long, floppy ears and a pink ribbon on her neck. She'd come with me to the U.K. and then across the ocean to Canada. No matter how many different beds I'd slept in, I'd had her pressed against my cheek. She was still in my closet, nestled among blankets and sweaters. I could never, ever let Bibi go, even if I didn't sleep with her anymore. I translated what Mr. Letner had said, but Amira shook her head.

"Did you ever have one?" I asked.

"Yes. But I gave him to a little girl in the camps. Her father had died. She had nothing and needed it more than I did." Amira stared at me with honey-brown eyes. I blinked and looked away. I'd never thought of Bibi sitting in my closet as a luxury, but to Amira, she probably was.

"Can I go next?" Allan stood up before Mr. Letner could argue. "Mr. Letner." He pointed to the screen, tapping it impatiently, thrilled to treat Mr. Letner as his assistant. Some of his friends snickered. Mr. Letner raised an eyebrow and gave him a warning look.

What came up on the screen was not what I'd expected. I thought he'd show a picture of himself mooning the camera. The photo was of Allan, but he was carrying someone in his arms. The boy's head hung back, his mouth slack, gangly arms and legs dangling. Allan's voice changed as he spoke. "This is my brother Cody. He has cerebral palsy, which means he can't do a lot of things on his own, like eat and walk, or even talk. The thinking part of his brain works fine, just not the parts that control his body." Allan's words came slowly as he looked at the photo, taking it in the way we were.

"He has a chair, like a motorized wheelchair, and sleeps on the main floor. But, uh, since my dad left, he hasn't been to my room because it's up the stairs and my mom and I aren't strong enough to carry him." He paused. "Until yesterday." He turned to the class. "That's what this picture is: me carrying Cody up to my room. First time he's been upstairs in three years."

The class was silent. We stared at the photo and this side of Allan we didn't know existed. Even Mr. Letner didn't say anything for a few minutes. Allan stood in front of us, shifting from side to side. "You have a title for this picture?" Mr. Letner finally asked. His voice was thick.

"Yeah, I want to call it *Strong*. Not cuz of me, but cuz of Cody. It's hard to be him, but he never complains." The class stayed quiet as Allan went back to his seat.

Amira tugged on my sleeve. I turned to her, wishing I didn't have to translate right now. But that wasn't what she wanted. "Will you help me to show my photo?" she asked.

"You want to show it to everyone?" I asked, frowning. What if she got to the front and froze, too scared to continue?

She nodded. "Isn't that the assignment?"

I raised my hand. "Mr. Letner, Amira wants to go next."

"Okay, great!" It was easy to hear the surprise in his voice. Most of the other kids had never heard her speak; some wouldn't even have remembered her name. I translated as she explained to Mr. Letner which photo she wanted to use. "That one!" she exclaimed as he flicked through what she'd uploaded to the computer. We moved to the front of the class.

The photo was actually of another photo. It was distorted and grainy, the colour faded. Three girls stood arm in arm, wearing school uniforms of white short-sleeved shirts and green skirts. They all had toothy grins, their hair wavy and curled. The girl in the middle was Amira, but she looked different. Rounded cheeks, laughter in her eyes; she was a shadow of that person now. Around her neck was a gold medal and it glinted in the sun.

She spoke quickly in Arabic, pointing to things in the photo as I listened and then translated for the class. "These were my friends in Homs. Our school is there." She pointed to a low building in the background. "This day was our track and field competition for lower school. I won a race and that is my medal. I don't have it anymore. I had to leave it behind.

"My friends left Homs before I did. I carried this picture with me to ask people if they'd seen them. It's one of the only things I still have from my old life. My only way to remember them. It's my most special thing."

Seeing her photo on the screen, a replica of the real thing, was sort of like looking at Amira now. The girl on the screen was full of life, joyful and carefree. The war hadn't started yet. All that mattered on that day was having fun with her friends. Would she have done anything different if she had known it would be the last photo she'd have of all of them together? I wanted to tell the kids in the class about how she'd given away her stuffy and that she couldn't use the playground in Homs because there were bombs planted around it.

Did that laughing girl still exist? I wondered. After everything that had happened to her, had the real Amira, the one in the photo, been erased? Or was she still inside, hiding?

CHAPTER 11

The buzzer had barely sounded for the end of the day when I took off from Math class and race-walked down the hallway to the gym doors to see if the tournament team roster was posted. A mass of kids clumped together in front of a typed piece of paper. I was too far back to read it. Allan pushed his way through and his voice rang out. "Yes!" he shouted with a fist pump. "Made it!"

But seeing a couple of kids leave with long faces got me worried. Would I be one of them? My play during the scrimmages had been good, but I wasn't the tallest or the fastest. What if it came down to me or a girl who was an inch taller? Josh turned from the list and raised his hand for a high-five. "We both made it!"

"I did?" A relieved smile stretched across my face.

"Told you, you would."

The look he gave me lasted a second too long. Not that I minded, but I could feel a blush spreading under my hijab. "What about Jillian? Which other girls made it?" I asked to turn the conversation back to the team.

"Jillian did. I'm not sure who else."

I let the news sink in.

"Guess I'll see you at practice tomorrow," he said. He gave me a grin that was impossible not to return. He lowered his voice. "About yesterday —"

My breath caught in my throat and I groaned. "Can we forget about it, please?"

He shifted his backpack on his shoulder as a kid behind him jostled him. "It's just" — he struggled for words — "you said some things. Like Mariam liking me? What's that all about?"

The blush deepened as I twisted my mouth. "I shouldn't have said that."

He raised his eyebrows, waiting for more of an explanation. "I like Mariam," he said. My stomach dropped. "As a friend. Same with Jill, if it matters."

It does! "Allan said something," I started to explain. "Well, I overheard him saying something ..." I let my voice drift off, hoping Josh would fill in the blanks.

"To you?"

He doesn't even remember? I swallowed, the awkwardness of the situation making me sweat. "Not exactly."

Josh waved his hand dismissively. "I don't listen to half of what Allan says and you shouldn't either. Sometimes it's easier to just agree with him." Was that what had happened? Had Josh agreed with Allan instead of arguing with him? It didn't make it right, but it did take some of the sting out of what I'd heard.

"Don't mention what I said about Mariam, okay? I should have kept my mouth shut."

Josh gave me a confused look. "You said what about who?" And then he grinned. "So, we're good?"

I nodded. "All good."

"I hated thinking you were mad at me," he confessed. *And I hated being mad at you.*

As Josh walked away, I pushed my way closer to the gym doors to read all the names. I scanned them to see who else had made it. Jillian, Ally, Sarah, Jeein, and me were the girls and Josh, Allan, Thomas, Mohammed, Shane, Casey, and Rory were the boys. I shared an excited smile with Shane, a new kid who had won the three-point shootout we'd had last tryout. He'd sunk ten in a row, which beat Josh by two.

"So, did you make it?" Mariam stood behind me. She had changed back into her hijab, hair tucked away, makeup scrubbed off. She looked like my friend again, but my guard was up. "Good for you." She sounded sincere.

I nodded, eyeing her warily. "Thanks."

"I mean it. I know how much it means to you. It's a big deal."

Now I was really suspicious. This was the most she'd talked to me all week. The crowd by the doors had thinned out. Just a few stragglers were still looking at the list. I pulled her to the side so I could talk to her quietly. "Mariam, what's going on?"

"What do you mean?"

"You've been ignoring me all week."

She shrugged like she hadn't noticed anything. "No, I haven't."

"Yeah, you have. If it's about Josh —"

She opened her eyes wide and gave me an incredulous stare. "Why did you bring his name up?" she whispered. *Because you acted like a jealous girlfriend a few days ago,* was what I wanted to say, but before I could even open my mouth, she was hissing in my face. "I was trying to be *nice*, but obviously all you care about is rubbing it in my face that you made the team and Josh likes *you*."

"What?" I looked at her, confused. "I'm not rubbing it in your face. You didn't even try out. And as for Josh —"

"I liked him first!"

I stared at her in disbelief. "*You liked him first?*" I repeated. "Are you serious?"

"I don't know how we were ever friends."

I blinked at her, wondering if I'd heard her right. Was I being tricked? I wanted to look around and check for a camera in case someone was videotaping this as a joke. Was Mariam actually letting a guy who neither of us could date come between us? A guy who had told me he only liked her as a friend?

"Oh my God!" Carmina appeared, breathless. "I just saw Daniel," she gasped. "He looked right at me and smiled!" Her face split into a grin, and as much as I wanted to share in the excitement of a boy *looking* at her, I wasn't in the mood. "Are you guys ready?" Carmina asked, eyeing us. She paused. The tension must have been obvious. "Are you coming to Mariam's?" she asked me.

"Uh, no. I can't today," I mumbled, looking anywhere but at Mariam. *Mainly because my supposed best friend didn't invite me.* Mariam refused to look at me and a hot swell of hurt rose in my chest.

"Okay," Carmina said, cringing at the awkwardness. "We're going to miss the bus," Carmina said to Mariam and gave me an apologetic look.

"Well, I'm ready to go," Mariam replied, brushing past me as if I was a nuisance that could be pushed aside.

I watched the two of them leave, trying to make sense of things. Up until recently, I'd thought I was Mariam's best friend. She'd liked Carmina, but they didn't share what we did. Then Mariam took off her hijab, and all of a sudden, I was nothing to her, and Carmina and she were best friends. I could understand wanting to have different friends, but I didn't understand why I was being pushed aside or why she wanted to hurt me. I took a deep breath and blinked away the tears welling in my eyes. As I passed the classroom door, I caught sight of myself in the small pane of glass. Was it the hijab that Mariam was running away from? Seeing me must remind her of who she really was, who she'd always be. I wished she'd realize that taking off her hijab wasn't going to change that.

"If we hadn't left Syria when we did, what would have happened to us?" I asked Mom and Dad at dinner. Aazim sat across from me, taking a break from his studying to shovel food into his mouth. Today was the first time all week he wasn't going back to school to study until ten or eleven o'clock at night. My parents liked that he was taking school seriously, but he was so exhausted that in the mornings, he'd sleep through his alarm. Mom had to turn on all the lights *and* threaten to dump a bucket of ice water on him to wake him up.

They both looked at me. "We would have left sooner or later," Dad said.

"But things got worse after we left," I pressed. "What if we'd stayed, like other people did?"

Mom pursed her lips. "Everyone made a choice. Lots of people believed the government wouldn't let things get as bad as they did, that they'd consider the people. We were lucky: your dad got a job and so much of our family was already in the U.K."

"What if he hadn't gotten a job, though? Would we have stayed?"

I could tell the conversation was making my parents uncomfortable. I'd been too young to *really* understand why we were leaving. I remembered crying myself to sleep the night our suitcases were lined up at the front door, ready for our departure the next morning. Everything else we were taking with us had already been boxed up and sent overseas. Mom had tried to make it sound like an adventure, but all I could think about was that I would never see my friends again.

Even Aazim took a break from eating to listen to Dad's answer. "By that point, we were committed to leaving. We were getting out one way or the other."

Mom said a quick prayer of thanks for our safe journey.

"Amira's told me things about what Syria is like now."

A knowing glance passed between them. "Yes, it's bad. Very bad."

"There's still people who can't leave."

"It's a war. That's what happens. Innocent people suffer," Aazim said. None of what they were saying was making me feel better. I'd been living my comfortable life in Canada, and even though my parents made sure we watched the news, it had been easy pretending that what was happening a world away in Syria didn't affect me. Amira's arrival had opened my eyes to the reality, and now I couldn't look away. It could just as easily have been me arriving with nothing but a photo of friends.

"It's hard to hear what's happening in Syria and not worry about friends and neighbours. People we knew," Mom said.

"Kids I went to school with, teachers," I said.

"Colleagues," Dad added.

I thought about the stuffie Amira had given away and her medals, maybe lost in rubble somewhere. We were both Syrian and both in Canada, but she'd had to endure so many bad things to get here. If Mariam and I weren't in a fight, these were the things I would have talked to her about, because she understood what it was like to leave people behind. For a while, things had gotten bad in Egypt, too. She'd been confused by tense phone calls between her parents and family who still lived there. But I couldn't talk to her. Not right now, anyway.

Mom reached across the table and held my hand. "This is not for you to feel guilty about."

I nodded again, but as long as I was friends with Amira, the reality of what she'd lived through would be there. In her haunted eyes and distant smile.

CHAPTER 12

I saw Mariam at her locker when I arrived at school and felt a knot tighten in my stomach. As I got closer, I kept an eye out for Carmina. I was still bothered about our argument and wanted to clear the air.

Mariam didn't even glance at me when I got to my locker, a few down from hers. I took a deep, determined breath. The bright pink tunic she was wearing made her skin glow. It was laced with gold thread and looked too fancy for a regular school day. Why did she bother dressing up if she was just going to change?

"I love your shirt," I said.

She gave me a cool look. "Thanks. I sewed it myself." Her words came through tight lips, but I could hear the pride in her voice.

"You did? It's really nice." I hated the gushy tone of my voice, but I couldn't help myself. I didn't know how else to make amends.

She pursed her lips. "I'm sick of all the boring clothes I have to wear. At least this way …" She let the conversation drift off. For as long as I'd known her, Mariam had been into clothes, but her sewing skills were obviously improving. I looked down at my outfit. An old T-shirt of Aazim's over a long-sleeved shirt and soccer pants wasn't exactly fashion forward.

"I'm sorry about yesterday."

She sighed. "Yeah, me, too."

It felt a little like it used to between us, like I had a one-inch opening. If I could just squeeze the rest of me through, maybe she'd see I wasn't the enemy. I was still her best friend. "Maybe we could hang out this weekend?"

"Hey, Sadia! Team practice at lunch today!" Josh called out as he walked past. I closed my eyes, wondering if Josh's timing could be any worse.

The corners of Mariam's mouth turned down in a frown. "Actually, there's a party I'm going to. With Carmina."

I stared at her, letting her words sink in. *A party?* "Really?"

She took my reply as a challenge. "Yeah," she said.

"Does it last all weekend?" I asked, more snarky than I intended. Even if she was going to the party, it didn't mean her whole weekend was booked.

Mariam narrowed her eyes. "Yeah. It does," she said sarcastically and turned on her heels.

I wanted to ask her how she was going to ask for permission, because we both knew her parents would never let her go. There had been plenty of things they'd said no to before. I doubted they would say yes to a party — especially if it was at someone's house they didn't know.

Unless she wasn't going to ask for permission.

I kept thinking her rebellion was just a phase and she'd snap out of it, but maybe I was wrong. Maybe

Mariam *wanted* to be the type of girl who de-jabbed and snuck out to go to parties. Her parents' plan to protect her with strict rules was going to backfire.

Amira found her way to class and sat down beside me. A few minutes later, Miss McKay, the resource teacher, came to get her for some intensive English lessons. She gave Amira a bright smile. "Should we go?" she asked.

Amira nodded, probably grateful to be in a room without twenty-eight kids speaking in rapid-fire English.

Once Amira left, our desk felt unbalanced. The dynamics had shifted between Carmina, Mariam, and me, and now I was the third wheel, the odd man out. I shifted my books to the edge of the desk and sat as far from Mariam as I could. On the board, Mr. Letner had written a new phrase: *Rule of Thirds.*

"Anyone want to take a guess at what this means?" he asked.

I glanced around. No one's hand went up. "It's a photography term," Mr. Letner said. He pulled up an image of a kid biking down a gravel road. "Do you see how the subject of the picture is in the bottom right-hand corner of the photograph? Most of the picture is taken up by the trees." He went to his computer and pressed a key. A grid of nine squares appeared on top of the photograph. "What do you notice if the photo is divided up like this?"

From behind me, someone mumbled, "I thought this was Global Issues, not a photography class!"

Franca's hand went up. "The boy only takes up one third of the photo."

Mr. Letner nodded. "Right. So for your next photos, think about perspective and —" He turned to the board and wrote *Composition*. "Think about the rule of thirds. Play around with how you put the picture together." He showed us a few examples of other photos that had used the rule of thirds. Once I knew to look for it, the rule was obvious. Rather than putting the main subject of the photo in the middle, dividing the picture up into thirds made it more interesting. Instead of just seeing a boy biking, I was wondering where he was going on the road. "Following the rule of thirds is going to make your photos really stand out at the art show."

"Did you say art show?" Avery asked.

"Oh, did I?" Mr. Letner put on a fake surprised look, like he'd said too much.

"What art show?" Carmina was suddenly alert. She'd been chipping away at her nail polish as Mr. Letner had been talking about the rule of thirds.

"The photos we looked at yesterday proved to me that some of you really *thought* about what you were going to take pictures of. They weren't random, they mattered to you. Like the kids who took pictures in the If You Give a Kid a Camera project, you showed us your perspective of the world. So, I asked Ms. Richards if we could join her art students in the divisional art show. This year, it's at a gallery downtown."

There was an excited murmur, but also a few groans. Someone at the back, probably Zak, asked, "Do we have to?"

"No," Mr. Letner said. "But I want you to think about Allan's photograph. How many of you had seen that side of him?"

I twisted in my seat toward the back of the room. Instead of making a sarcastic comment, Allan was silently watching Mr. Letner. The only hand that went up to answer the question was Josh's.

"How many of you thought his photograph was powerful?" This time, every hand went up, even Zak's. "These photographs are your perspective, your voice."

"What if we don't have anything to say?" Mariam mumbled. I looked at her, wondering if she realized how ironic her question was. Of everyone in the class, she was the one saying something — every time she took off her hijab. It was like a shout right in my face.

I tried not to think about Mariam for the rest of the morning. I avoided her at lunch and sat with the girls who'd made the basketball team. It wasn't until she showed up in the gym at basketball practice that I was forced to face her.

At first, I thought she was there to smooth things over with me, but as she marched past me and went straight to Mr. Letner, I realized I was wrong.

"Hey, everyone!" Mr. Letner called. "Bring it in for a second." We all stopped what we were doing to make a semicircle in front of him. "Mariam has offered to help manage the team."

I gritted my teeth at Mariam's sudden interest in basketball. I wondered if she was only offering so she could keep an eye on Josh. What did she know about managing a team? "She'll be checking attendance at practices, organizing the schedule, and looking after the uniforms. There's also the permission forms for the tournament. They need to be returned to her by next week so I can submit the official roster."

My spirits sank as a satisfied smile spread across Mariam's face. I knew she had no interest in basketball; she'd said so herself. She was offering to help for the wrong reasons. If our argument kept going, it would make things awkward on the bench. I didn't want to be distracted when I needed to focus on playing.

I don't know if it was having Mariam in the gym, the way that she was smiling at Josh, or that my hijab kept coming loose, but I had a terrible practice. None of my balls went in the net. Anytime a pass came my way, I found a way to flub it up, dropping the ball, bumping into a teammate. I fouled out twice when we were scrimmaging. But I couldn't take a breather because it meant sitting on the bench with Mariam.

"Everything okay, Sadia?" Mr. Letner asked me on a water break. "Your timing's off today."

"I know," I groaned.

He looked like he wanted to say something else. "Can I talk to you over here?" He gestured for me to follow him into the gym teacher's office. *It's about Mariam*, I thought. He can tell there's something going on between us. Maybe he'd go back on his decision to let her be team manager if he knew it didn't sit well with me.

"This is a sensitive topic," he began, "and I don't want you to be offended. Your head scarf, it might be a problem during the tournament. The rules are pretty clear that players aren't allowed to wear head coverings. I've emailed the organizers to see if they'll allow an exception."

I stared at him. "I can't take it off."

"I know. And hopefully, this will all get cleared up." Mr. Letner wrinkled his forehead. "I didn't want to upset you, but I thought you should know, just in case. We'll wait and see what they say, okay? The tournament is still a few weeks away."

"If they don't let me play, it's discrimination," I said. "Wearing hijab is part of my religion. This is Canada! Everyone in Canada is equal. I should get to play like the other kids, no matter what I'm wearing." My cheeks flushed with indignation.

"I know," Mr. Letner nodded. "The rule book states that it's a safety issue."

Even as I stood in the office fuming, I thought of when Abby had hit me on the nose. If I hadn't been wearing my hijab, I would have seen her elbow coming. But kids got hurt accidentally all the time; it wasn't a reason to make me go against my religious beliefs.

The bell rang for afternoon classes. Mr. Letner peeked into the gym. Kids tossed their balls into the bin and ran to get changed. "As soon as I find out their decision, I'll let you know."

I stormed out of the gym and barrelled into Mariam as she made her way, slowly, to class. "Ow! Watch it!" She rubbed her shoulder where we'd collided. Then she took a look at my face. "What's wrong?" she asked.

"You wouldn't care if I told you."

She pursed her lips.

But it all came spilling out, anyway. Because of all people, Mariam *would* understand. "Mr. Letner said I might not be able to play in the tournament unless I take off my hijab. They have rules about head coverings."

Mariam's eyes widened in surprise. "That's not fair. It's not for fashion, we're Muslim."

"What if I can't play?" I wailed. After all my hard work to make the team, I couldn't stand the thought of being kicked off for a stupid rule.

Mariam put a consoling hand on my arm. "They've probably never had a girl in hijab play before. They'll realize what they're doing is unfair." It felt good to have her on my side, like a crack in the wall between us was opening. "You know, you *could* take it off."

I shirked away from her. "No, I couldn't."

She rolled her eyes. "It's probably just for one game. An hour of your life."

"That's not even the point." The hall emptied as kids around us made their way to class. "What happens next year when I want to play again? I'll have to keep taking it off. And it might not be for just one hour. We could make it to the quarter-finals and the semis. Maybe even further. What about other girls who want to play? Are we all supposed to take off our hijab for *their* rules?"

"Okay, don't get so worked up. I'm on your side, remember?"

I frowned at her. Was she? Maybe she was enjoying this. Without me on the team, she would have Josh all to herself, which was what she'd wanted all along.

"Girls! Get to class, please." Mrs. Marino speed-walked down the hall, not stopping as she breezed past us. For a little lady, she could motor when she had to. Her hair bounced behind her. Mariam and I went to our lockers to get books for our afternoon classes. When I sat down for English, Amira smiled at me, but I didn't have it in me to return the greeting.

"What's wrong?" she asked. When I explained about the tournament rules, she frowned.

"You can't take off your hijab," she said, shaking her head.

"I also can't *not* play in the tournament."

Amira shot me a look and I knew the choice wouldn't be so hard for her. Was it because I'd lived in Canada longer that I was conflicted? I knew my parents would agree with Amira. If I took it off for the basketball games, what would stop me from being like Mariam and removing it at school, or whenever it was inconvenient? There were lots of times when it would be easier to blend in with everyone else. I thought of the lady on the bus. She wouldn't have given me a second glance if I hadn't been wearing my hijab.

But then I wouldn't be me. And my religion was a big part of who I was. I spent the rest of the afternoon torn between my options. I'd been judging Mariam for taking off her hijab to fit in, but now I was considering doing the same so I could play basketball. Picking and choosing when I wore it would make me a huge hypocrite.

Maybe I was stressing for nothing. Maybe the tournament organizers would realize their rule was discriminatory and change it. I mean, this was Canada!

CHAPTER 13

The door to the washroom opened and then closed with a muffled thud. We'd started the day with our first early morning practice. Mr. Letner had worked us hard and we still had a scrimmage scheduled at lunch. I was sweating in places I didn't know could sweat.

After washing my face in the washroom sink and tidying myself up as best I could before class started, I went into a stall. I wasn't expecting anyone to come in to the washroom. The bell for morning classes hadn't rung yet.

Then from under the stall door, I saw Mariam's shoes and heard her school bag hit the countertop. *Ugh.* Of course, she'd need to come in here to de-jab herself. Should I make a noise so she'd know she wasn't alone? I'd taken a stall a few from the end, and when I peeked through the crack between the stall door and the frame, I had a view of Mariam and her reflection in the mirror.

She was giving herself a long, hard look, like she was trying to remember the details of her face. She screwed up her mouth, her brow wrinkling with frustration, and pulled back her hijab. I watched as she shook her head and let the scarf fall to the counter. I'd thought she'd be gleeful removing it, but what I saw confused me. She looked as upset about it as I would have been. She took off her tunic next — not the one I'd complimented her on before, but another one that she may have sewn herself. It had an asymmetrical hem and matched the bright turquoise of her head scarf. Underneath, she wore a T-shirt, a name-brand logo emblazoned on the front. She brushed out her hair, letting it fall in waves over her shoulders and back.

It was too late now to emerge from the stall. There'd be too much awkwardness. I'd have to wait here until she left. Someone else entered and I heard a *hey*, from Carmina. She said it in her usual singsong way, drawing it out. Instantly, Mariam's stance changed. Any conflict she felt about taking off her hijab was hidden the moment Carmina came into the washroom.

"Hey," she responded. The two of them stood side by side as Carmina pulled out her makeup bag. I was stuck in the stall listening to them rifle through brushes and plastic cases as they painted their faces. Mariam had moved beyond just lip gloss. Eye shadow, mascara, and eyeliner all went on, then blush and lipstick. She looked like a painted doll when she was done.

"Are you excited for the party?" Carmina asked. I listened intently, curious to know more.

There was hesitation in Mariam's voice. Carmina might not have been able to hear it, but I'd known Mariam as a best friend for years. "I might not be able to go," she said.

"What? Why?"

"My parents are lame. They don't know your parents, so they probably won't let me sleep over."

"No," Carmina whined. "You have to come! It's going to be so fun! Everyone's going, Josh, Allan, Avery, tons of people from our homeroom. Daniel will be there, too!"

"I know," Mariam answered in the same whiney tone.

"Say you're going to someone else's house then," Carmina suggested.

My breath caught in my throat. She'd ask me. I was the logical choice. She'd slept over at my house lots of times, and her parents wouldn't suspect anything out of the ordinary. "I *could* say I'm going to Sadia's," Mariam said.

"Yeah," Carmina said, excited. "She could come, too —"

"No. Her parents would never allow it." My heart shrivelled at the deception. My *parents would never allow it?* I wanted to scream at her. How would she know? It took every bit of self-control not to burst out of the washroom stall and confront her. But if I did, it would only make me look bad because I'd been snooping on her.

I waited while they packed up their makeup and clothes, giggling and talking about homework and teachers and boys. When they'd left and the door had closed after them, I came out of the stall and walked to the sink. I stared at myself. What would it be like to take off the hijab and expose my hair and neck for everyone to see?

I could play basketball unencumbered. I could take the bus without anyone staring. I could be like almost everyone else at school.

But, I couldn't do it. My hijab was part of me; turning away from it meant denying who I was.

I needed to face the facts. My best friend was moving beyond me. She was going to places that I couldn't follow, down a path that I didn't *want* to follow. Maybe I just had to let her go.

When I got to homeroom, I slid into my seat as if I hadn't just overheard her conversation with Carmina in the washroom. When she nudged me after "O Canada," while we were supposed to be listening to announcements, I knew what she was going to ask before she pushed the note my way. "Still want to hang out this weekend?" she'd written on the corner of her paper. I stared at it and met her innocent gaze. She looked at me, eyebrows raised.

She was using me. I wasn't a friend, I was a means to get where she really wanted to be. The knowledge hurt, like toes pinched tight in shoes. It wouldn't cripple me, but I wished I didn't have to feel it. Saying yes was agreeing to her deceit.

But I did. I took my pencil and drew a smiley face. She grinned back at me.

I tightened my hijab around my neck. The lunchtime scrimmage had gotten more aggressive because Mr. Letner had warned us that some of the other teams in the tournament played rough. He wanted us to push back and practise like we were going for the jugular. Twice my head scarf had come loose, the ends swinging down and almost unravelling. Sweat beaded across my forehead and I could feel it dripping down my temples. I was on the bench, waiting to be subbed back in. Jillian knew how to use her body, pushing her elbow out just far enough to avoid fouling the other player. I didn't have her size, but my speed meant I could dart in for a quick pass in the key. It also meant I was in the middle of the action with hands and arms flying. My hijab was becoming a hindrance. I understood why wearing it would be a problem at the tournament.

Mariam had been friendlier since I'd agreed to "hang out" on the weekend. I wished I could tell her that I knew about her ulterior motive. We were lying to each other, pretending to be something we weren't anymore.

Mr. Letner tapped me on the shoulder as Ally ran off. We slapped hands as I went on the court. Everyone was breathing hard, giving their all, and pretending that this wasn't a practice. We were playing like one of the other teams was with us in the gym. I had the ball and was looking for an opening when Jillian fouled me so hard I went flying and landed on my butt. I lay on the ground, stunned. Mr. Letner didn't have to blow his whistle for the play to stop. Josh held out his hand to me. "Okay?" he asked as he hauled me up.

I nodded. One side of my scarf was covering my face. The other side was probably hanging over my shoulder. With a frustrated groan, I marched to the bench and knelt beside Mariam. "Can you fix it?" I asked. She had to be quick because the teams were waiting for me to take the foul shot.

She put aside her clipboard and smoothed back my hair. "Ew," she said. "You're sweaty." With quick fingers, she pulled the bonnet cap forward and then tightened my scarf. "Done." I caught sight of Mr. Letner. He was frowning and I could guess why. In a game, my hijab could cost the team if I had to call a time out or get subbed out to fix it.

"Thanks." I jumped up and took my spot on the free-throw line. Josh bounced the ball to me. I steadied my nerves. The hoop smiled down at me. *Put the ball in the hoop*, I told myself. I took a breath, raised the ball over my head, and let it sail in an arc to the basket. It *swoosh*ed into the net. As long as I could keep scoring, Mr. Letner would do what he had to, to keep me on the team. "Nice!" Allan said and gave me a quick high-five before we both ran downcourt.

I sat out the last shift, watching the scrimmage. Mariam shifted closer to me and nudged my elbow. She pointed with her pen to a sketch of a girl wearing a hijab. "Look," she said. "What do you think?"

Bending closer, I saw that it wasn't an ordinary hijab. The scarf wasn't loose. It wrapped tightly around the head and hung down to cover the neck, fitting close to the body. The outfit underneath was different, too: long pants and a shirt, close fitting but not tight. On top she'd drawn our school basketball jersey, but with a band across the bottom to make it long enough to hit mid-thigh. "Is that a uniform?" I asked.

"Yeah. *Your* uniform. I can't handle watching your scarf fly off anymore. Plus, you look so hot. And not in a good way."

I was. Sweat collected at the nape of my neck and trickled down my back.

"I could sew it out of that breathable athletic fabric. You'd be cooler *and* look more like the rest of the team. I could use blue for the pants and grey for the shirt."

It took a second for her words to register. "You're going to sew it?"

Mariam looked at me. I knew she was good at making clothes, but this was a whole uniform. "Isn't it complicated?"

"B-but," I stuttered, confused. "You can sew that well?"

She pursed her lips and gave me a look filled with attitude. "You've seen the stuff I make. What do you think?"

I had no idea how hard, or how easy, it was to sew what she'd drawn, so I picked a safe option and nodded. I looked at the sketch again. She'd labelled different things on it, like the type of fabric and notes for herself: "Put thumbhole in sleeve" and "drawstring waist."

"It's really good," I said, trying to cover my surprise at how talented she was.

"Thanks. I'm going to work on it this weekend. Maybe you can try on a sample on Monday."

"If we're hanging out this weekend ..." I let my words drift off.

"Oh, right! I can take measurements! That's perfect," her face lit up, which left me confused. Maybe she wasn't using me after all.

Mr. Letner blew his whistle in two short blasts. Game over. Mariam was supposed to be keeping score, but her attention had drifted away from the game and to the sketch. Everyone looked at her for an announcement of who had won. "Fifty-four to fifty-one, for Jillian's team," I whispered to her.

"Fifty-four to fifty-one, for Jillian's team," she repeated. Jillian nodded and fist-bumped her teammates. I ran to join the end-of-game lineup and the chorus of "Good game. Good game," as we snaked past each other.

"Sorry about the push," Jillian said to me as we walked to the change room.

I shrugged it off. "Part of the game."

"Yeah. Sometimes I get too into it."

"Good thing we're on the same team for the tournament."

Jillian grinned at me and pushed open the door to the change room. It was humid in there, even with only five girls. Our chatter echoed off the walls. I ran the water at the sink until it was at its coldest and then splashed it on my face, not caring about how wet my hijab got. Could Mariam really sew me something more comfortable? Two years ago, Aazim and I had played basketball with abandon in the driveway. Without my hijab, I'd been able to run, shoot, and dribble unencumbered. I said a silent prayer that Mariam was as good a designer as she thought she was.

When I got home from school, Mom was in the kitchen. She didn't look up when I walked in but continued to chop an onion so violently that I couldn't resist asking, "What did it do to you?"

"Nothing," she replied tersely, not in the mood for a joke.

"You okay?"

She didn't answer, but it was clear she *wasn't* okay. Her mouth was pinched tight and her eyebrows were drawn together in a frown. "Mom?"

She paused in mid-chop, gripping the knife, trying to keep her emotions in check.

"What's wrong?"

"Nothing. Never mind."

"Wasn't today your first day volunteering at the library?" I asked, clueing in to why she might be upset. "Did something happen?"

She took a deep breath. "Not at the library. After, when I was waiting for the bus," Mom said reluctantly. "A man yelled at me to go home from his car window and threw his cigarette at me."

My breath caught in my throat. "Are you serious?" One look at her face gave me the answer. "Are you okay? Did you get burned?"

She shook her head. "It isn't the first time something like this has happened, it's just —" she broke off, her voice cracking. "I'd had such a good day. I felt useful. People came in and needed my help, and then when I left the library, excited to share my day with my family, *that* happened. I was so embarrassed. All the people at the bus stop ..." Her voice drifted off.

My throat got tight as I watched her hold herself together. Was this part of being Muslim? Facing racism and learning to deal with it? Dad would be furious when he found out, but there was nothing he could do. He was as powerless as Mom had been.

"I was shaking, I was so upset. And then a woman came up to me." Mom took a shuddering breath. "She said if I wanted to stay in Canada, I should be Canadian and stop dressing like a terrorist." Her lips trembled and she put a hand to her mouth. She tried to hold the sobs back, but couldn't.

I stared at her, shocked that someone could say something so hateful to a person they didn't know.

"I wish I'd said something to that woman," she muttered. "But I was so humiliated, I just walked away. Like a mouse." She gave up trying to compose herself. She wiped her eyes and got a tissue to blow her nose.

"What could you have said? She wouldn't have listened," I argued.

"I got tongue-tied. The English words wouldn't come." Mom's expression changed, her face hardened, as she lashed out in virulent Arabic, telling the woman what she could do with her misguided opinion of Muslims.

I thought about the woman who'd been staring at me on the bus. Maybe I should have said something to her — nothing rude, but if we talked, she'd see I was more than a head scarf. So was Mom.

I wondered if kids at school harboured racist ideas. No one had said anything to me, but I remembered the looks we got from some people when Mariam and I had started wearing hijab.

As Mom went back to cooking dinner, I pulled out my phone and typed out a message to Mariam. If there was anyone who would understand what it was like to see my mom crying because of hurtful, racist comments, it was her. I stared at what I'd written, my thumb hovering over the send button. What if it just gave her more reason not to wear her hijab? A few other families at our mosque were telling their daughters not to because they worried about their safety.

I didn't want to get into an argument about it with her. And lately, I wasn't very good at predicting where a conversation would go. I deleted the message and didn't know what felt worse: watching Mom deal with the hurtful comments, or not being able to tell my best friend about it.

CHAPTER 14

I sat distracted in class as Mr. Letner talked about the global effects of rising water levels. I kept tuning in and out because my mind was on my mom and the incident at the bus stop yesterday. I still hadn't said anything about it to Mariam. As much as I wanted to, her de-jabbing had put up a wall between us. I could have told the old Mariam, but I didn't know if the newer, de-jabbed version would want to listen.

Mr. Letner wrapped up the discussion. "We have some time, does anyone want to show a photo?"

No one raised their hand right away. When Mom had told Dad about the bus stop after dinner, I'd retreated to my room with the school camera. I knew Dad wouldn't fly into a rage, but I imagined the simmering anger that he'd feel and didn't want to be around to see it.

Upstairs, I'd played around with lighting, angles, and the rule of thirds to get a different perspective of a basketball. The challenge of taking an artistic photo was a good distraction. After trial and error, I'd finally captured the shot I wanted: half the ball was covered in shadow, and the light from my desk lamp illuminated the bumpy surface on the other side.

"Anyone?" Mr. Letner asked again and scanned the room, waiting. I could feel his eyes on me and wasn't surprised when he called me up to the front. I showed him where to find the photo, but he accidentally opened a different one in my folder. A photo of the prayer mat at my house popped up. I'd lain down to take the picture, so the carpet stretched out in front. Only the closest swirling pattern of colours and fringed edges were in focus, the rest of it was blurred.

"Tell us about this, Sadia."

"Uh, well, it's not a basketball," I said, caught off guard.

"*Sajada*." Amira blurted out the Arabic word for prayer rug.

I grinned at her and she smiled back. When I'd first come to Canada, everything had been so foreign. Any flash of familiarity had been comforting.

"It's called a *sajada* in Arabic, like Amira said. It's a prayer rug. We use it five times a day to pray."

Mr. Letner nodded at me to continue, but I was self-conscious talking about prayers with the class. I wished I could sit down instead of explaining it. "It gets rolled up after we use it," I said, noticing how frayed the edges were, threads escaping the binding. "We pray facing Mecca, our holy place," I explained. I thought I'd look out into the class and see everyone's eyes glazed over. But they were all paying attention, interested in what I had to say.

"Why did you choose to photograph it?" Mr. Letner asked.

I looked at the picture on the Smartboard behind me. I almost took the easy way out and shrugged, but I caught a glimpse of Amira, sitting up straight and straining to make sense of what I was saying in English. And I thought about Mom. If the woman who'd been rude to her had known a little more about Islam, maybe she wouldn't have stereotyped Mom into being a terrorist. "I wanted to look at it from a different perspective, like you said."

"But why take a photo of a prayer mat at all? There are probably lots of things in your house that you could have photographed close up like that."

He was right. Why had I chosen the prayer rug? "We brought it from Syria when we moved. I remember it being in our living room in Damascus. I guess it's like a connection between those two places."

A lot of kids didn't know I was Syrian. Only the ones who had been at my middle school would have remembered. I saw a few of them perk up with curiosity.

"Any questions?" Mr. Letner asked the class. Some hands went up.

"Why don't you pray at school?"

"I'm supposed to." I looked out at their curious faces. "Even though we have a room we can use for midday prayers" — I glanced at Mohammed — "it's hard sometimes to fit it in."

"Where's Mecca?"

Before I could answer, Allan piped up with: "Why do you wear that thing on your head?"

Mariam turned around in her seat. "It's not a *thing*, Allan. It's a hijab, a head covering. A woman's hair must be covered, according to the Qur'an." Mariam's voice faded as she spoke. She knew what his next question was going to be.

"Why don't you wear yours?" he asked her.

I bit my lip waiting for her response.

"It's a personal choice," she replied and turned around in her desk.

"Did you leave before the war?" Riley asked quietly. He looked at me with curiosity, as if he had more questions but was too shy to ask them.

"Uh, yeah, we did."

"So, you weren't a refugee?"

I shook my head. "No." I couldn't help but glance at Amira.

Mr. Letner stood up and nodded for me to sit down. I wondered if he wanted to avoid any more talk of refugees with Amira in the room. "Thank you, Sadia. Anyone else want to show their photos?"

We spent another thirty minutes looking at photos. Some were of pets and others followed Zander's theme of childhood toys. Franca's photo was of her grandmother cooking in the basement of her house. She wore a stained apron over her dress and slippers. The pots on the stove bubbled with tomato sauce; pasta packages and empty cans littered the counter. I could almost smell the meal. "She's making a lasagna for our whole family, all sixteen of us, and she's eighty-four!" Franca went on to tell us that her grandpa died when her dad was twelve and her grandma, nonna, had raised five boys on her own, working as a cook at an Italian restaurant. She still lived in the same house. "She's, like, the most amazing woman ever," Franca told us. "That's why I took this photo."

"Bet she makes a mean lasagna," Mr. Letner said.

"She does!"

"Who's next?" Mr. Letner asked. No one raised their hand, but his eyes fell on Josh. "Come on up," he said. Reluctantly, Josh left his desk and made his way to the front.

The picture that appeared on the Smartboard was of a man standing at rink level at a hockey game. His arm was raised and he was pointing at someone on the ice. He was yelling, his face red and contorted with anger or frustration, it was hard to tell which.

"Yeah, so ..." Josh shifted nervously, foot to foot.

"Who's in the picture?" Mr. Letner prompted him.

"That's my dad. He's watching my brother play hockey."

Josh looked at Mr. Letner, who nodded at him to continue. "Tell us why you took the photo."

"When you were talking about perspective, it got me thinking about what my brother and I see from the ice when we play. My dad has no idea how insane he looks. I know he loves hockey and 'crazy hockey dads,'" he held up his fingers in air quotes, "are part of the game, but sometimes, looking over and seeing him like this ..." He paused. "It's embarrassing." A couple of guys in the class made noises of agreement. "I wish the glass was a mirror so he could see what we see."

Mr. Letner gave Josh a long look. "Out of curiosity, are you going to show this picture to your dad?"

Josh glanced at the photo again and frowned. "I don't know," he sighed.

Sometimes my parents embarrassed me when I played, shouting or cheering too loudly, but they never argued with a ref or called out the other players. And they *never* looked as irate as Josh's dad.

Josh went back to his seat, and Mr. Letner said, "We have time for one more. Who's up?" Most kids had presented at least one photo. Mr. Letner scanned the room and his gaze fell on Mariam. She looked at her hands fidgeting under her desk. "Mariam, we haven't seen any of your photos yet. Care to share?"

She twisted her mouth like she was working up the courage to say yes. With a deep breath, she nodded and went to show Mr. Letner which photo to put on the Smartboard. Seeing her in front of the class, she looked petite, small-boned, and delicate. Her eyes flitted anxiously around the classroom. "This is a photo from my room." The picture that came up was of a bulletin board. Mariam had tacked up pages ripped out of magazines, pictures printed off the internet, and scraps of fabric. Some were even drawings she'd done of outfits. "This is my inspiration board." It was like a quilt of paper, covering every millimetre of the corkboard.

"Inspiration for what?" Mr. Letner peered closer at the computer screen in front of him.

"Designing. I want to be a fashion designer when I grow up." The words came out in a rush and were news to me. Although it did make sense. Carmina nodded and I started to wonder if a love of fashion was the thing that connected them. I'd been assuming Mariam was turning away from me because I reminded her of her old self, but maybe that wasn't it. Maybe she was moving *to* something that I didn't know anything about. I sat back in my chair, feeling further from her than ever.

"Cool," Mr. Letner smiled at her. "How do you decide what makes it up on the board?" he asked.

"Mostly I just choose pictures of outfits I like." A lot of them were ads for high-end name brands.

Mr. Letner pointed to a photo from a mosque. Taken from the back of the women's section, it showed a sea of colourful head scarves. "Tell me about that one."

"O-oh," Mariam stammered. "That one. I found it in a travel magazine. I put it up because I liked all the colours. It reminds me how beautiful prayers can be."

"Very cool," Mr. Letner said.

"There's also sketches of outfits I've designed. Ones I want to sew." She pointed a few out and waited for more questions.

"Who taught you to sew?"

"My mom. She sews her own clothes." I thought about Mrs. Hassanin and the stylish outfits she wore to the mosque. I had no idea she'd made them herself. "I'm —" Mariam caught herself and looked at me. "I'm going to try and sew a new basketball uniform for Sadia. One that's more comfortable."

I grinned with surprise. A small, determined smile spread across her face. From the corner of my eye, I saw Carmina smiling, too.

"Very cool," Mr. Letner said again. "This is turning into a passion project!" he said excitedly.

"A what?" Avery asked.

"A passion project, something you do on your own time."

"So, a hobby?" Zak said. There was a touch of cynicism in his voice, but Mr. Letner didn't let it deter him.

"No, more than a hobby. A passion project is something you work on because you want to, not because you have to." He looked at Allan. "When you showed us the photo of your brother, it got me thinking.... Maybe you could invent something to help him? That would be a passion project."

All eyes went to Allan, who frowned, thinking.

"So we're supposed to invent something?" A low murmur of confusion went through the room.

"Not necessarily. You might want to paint, or make music, or find an organization you want to volunteer with. A passion project can be anything *you* find interesting. But you have to push yourselves. Don't just play piano; write your own song and perform it for us. Want a better way to get to school? Invent an electric skateboard." He directed that idea at Zak, who stopped peeling a sticker off his binder to listen. "Or make a YouTube video to teach people your favourite tricks. Start an after-school class at the skate park for kids who want to learn." Zak sat up straighter at his desk, interested.

"How many marks is it worth?" Larissa asked.

"No marks."

No marks? "So why would we do it?" Zander asked, echoing my thoughts.

Mr. Letner waited a moment before answering. "A passion project is something you work on because you want to. It's not about marks."

"Josh, you talked about wishing our city could host an NBA game. You could look into what it takes, see if it's possible. Interview people, research what other cities have done to get expansion teams." He looked at me next. "Sadia, you'd have to help Mariam. She can sew, but you know what you need as a player." I looked at Mariam. She smiled at me and nodded. Mr. Letner looked at the class. "Anyone have any other ideas?" For a minute, it was quiet. Then Franca wondered if making a cookbook with her grandma's recipes was a passion project and Mr. Letner nodded.

"Maybe I could sell it to raise money for a charity," she said.

A slow smile spread across Mr. Letner's face. "Tell you what, kids who are interested in learning more, stay after class."

As the bell rang, about half the class packed up to leave. The rest of us, even Mariam, stayed in our seats. "Can I do something with art?" Avery asked. "Like drawing? Or taking pictures?"

"You could do the pictures of the food in the cookbook," Franca said as a joke, but Mr. Letner lifted one shoulder as if to say, Why not?

It was like the wheels in everyone's brains started to turn at the same time. Veronica had gone to the conservatory and taken photos of her favourite flowers, so she said she wanted to design a new garden for the schoolyard.

"Anyone like building things?" Mr. Letner asked, and Aidan's hand shot up. "You could make the containers for the garden."

"Or a birdhouse," Aidan suggested. Pretty soon, people were talking with their friends, coming up with ideas for a passion project. Carmina said she wanted to create a graphic novel with a Filipino main character.

"I hate that there aren't any books with characters who look like me," she explained.

Riley shyly added that he could write the story for it, if she wanted. When Carmina grinned at him and said yes, his cheeks turned so red, I thought they were going to ignite. I also saw the way Carmina's eyes lit up when Riley crouched at her desk to talk to her.

When the second bell rang, we ignored it because no one wanted to leave.

Except maybe Amira. I'd forgotten about her. She looked at me helplessly.

"What is going on?" she asked.

While everyone else had been coming up with ideas, she'd been sitting at the desk, confused. A little swell of guilt rose in me. I'd been in her shoes once.

"We're coming up with ideas for passion projects." There was no easy way to describe what Mr. Letner had assigned us — even though it wasn't really an assignment. We would be working on our projects on our own time, not at school, and they didn't count for marks.

I tried my best to explain everyone's projects to Amira, but she kept looking at me with a frown. "Do you get it?" I asked.

She nodded, but still looked confused, and I wondered if she was just faking it to avoid feeling clued out. I used to fake things all the time to fit in. I'd watch, take things in, and then try them out on my own. Sometimes, like throwing a snowball, they worked, but other times, taking a risk and acting like I knew what I was doing was a big, fat failure. How many times had I thought I understood a game in gym, only to embarrass myself?

Amira sat quietly, her brow furrowed as if she was concentrating on something. Maybe she understood more than I gave her credit for. After living in refugee camps for the last year and half, she'd proven that she was a survivor. There was no way high school was more challenging than the life she'd left behind.

CHAPTER 15

I hated to admit it, but the thought of Mariam coming over gave me butterflies of excitement. I'd gone from assuming our friendship was over to feeling a flicker of hope. It felt like a long time since we'd hung out.

She still hadn't admitted that the real reason she was coming over was to escape the watchful eyes of her parents and go to the party with Carmina. I'd play dumb, of course, when she did. A little piece of me hoped that maybe she'd change her mind and just want to stay at my house. Like old times, the two of us could stay up late watching movies and eating popcorn.

"Sadia!" Mom called from downstairs. "Mariam is here."

I raced down the stairs to the front door. She stood in her hijab with a bag in her hand and waved goodbye to her dad. He reversed out of our driveway and I shut the door. "Hi!" Her bag was stuffed with clothes — *borrowed from Carmina for the party?* I wondered — and a sleeping bag. Her sketchbook stuck out the top of it.

It was like falling back into our old ways; I led the way upstairs and Mariam followed. Mom watched us from the front entrance, smiling. "Dinner will be ready in half an hour. Did you eat, Mariam?"

"No."

"Good. You can join us."

Mariam grinned at me, something unspoken between us, like an agreement that things were back to normal now that we were in my house. "I brought a measuring tape so I can make the pattern for your uniform," she said, setting down her bag beside my bed. "Mom wouldn't let me bring the sewing machine." She rolled her eyes. "It would have been easier to sew it with you here."

"I can't believe you can do all this," I said, impressed.

She shrugged. "Guess there's some things even you don't know about me."

I didn't like the smugness of her words, but I let it go. I didn't want to ruin the evening. Mariam didn't waste any time. She whipped out the yellow measuring tape and wrapped it around me, taking note of my waist, hip, and chest measurements and then holding one end of it with her toe on the floor and reaching up to my waist. She wrote everything down on a piece of paper.

"I think I'll make your head covering first. That's the most important."

"It will be so good not to have to worry about it coming undone all the time. It drives me crazy."

Mariam's phone rang. She glanced at it lying on my bed. A photo of Carmina's face popped up. "I should get that," she said. There was a moment of awkwardness. She probably wanted me to give her privacy, but it was my room. I pretended to busy myself with the sketch of the uniform.

"Hi," she said into her phone. Carmina's echoey voice came back. Mariam moved to the far corner of my room and turned to the wall, but I could get the gist of the conversation from Mariam's responses. "Yeah, I'm still coming … I'm busy right now … No … Can I call you later?"

Mariam hung up and dropped her phone on my bed. "Okay, let's get to work," she said, as if the conversation had never happened. She pulled out a roll of fabric. So it wasn't clothes stuffed in her bag …

"Now?"

"Sure," she shrugged. "Why not?"

I didn't have a reason, other than I thought she was ditching me to hang out with Carmina and wouldn't want to start the project when she'd have to leave right away. I watched as she pulled out other things from her bag: sewing supplies and pattern envelopes. Inside the envelopes were pieces of tissue paper that had been folded and used many times. Pinholes dotted the edges. "I'm going to combine a few patterns to make the uniform. I'll start with this one." She showed me a knight's costume her mom had sewn for Halloween. "See the helmet? It'll work perfectly." The close-fitting head covering would hang over my neck.

She measured my head and pinned the pattern pieces she needed onto the fabric, being careful not to waste any. They fit snugly into one corner. "Okay, ready?" she asked, holding the scissors above the fabric. They slid open like the jaws of a shark.

"Ready!" She snipped the fabric, cutting around the outside of the tissue paper and laid each piece to the side.

"Okay, now, I'm going to unpin them and baste them

together so we can see if this will work." She took a deep breath. I'd never seen Mariam so focused on something.

"Dinner!" Mom called from downstairs. Mariam was halfway through creating the prototype and neither of us wanted to leave. In the mirror, I could see the head covering taking shape. I'd had to remove my usual scarf and bonnet cap and my hair lay flat after wearing it all day.

"Girls, dinner —" Mom opened the door to my room. She cut off her words as she took in the fabric and sewing supplies strewn around my room. "What's going on?"

"Mariam is making me a new basketball uniform," I said proudly.

"Yep," Mariam mumbled. She had three pins stuck between her lips and didn't look up as she spoke. "I made this, too," she said lifting a shoulder to indicate her tunic. Flimsy, black fabric matched her hijab. She had a long-sleeved shirt underneath it. Mariam surveyed the work so far in the mirror. She'd been pinning the underside to make sure it stayed snug on my head. Right now, it looked like a torture device from the Middle Ages, with pins sticking out at funny angles and the band stretching across my forehead.

"Hmmm," Mom said thoughtfully. "That's very industrious of you, Mariam. Dinner's ready." Mom gave us a thoughtful look, a hint of a smile on her lips, and went downstairs. Mariam looked at me in the mirror. Her green eyes shifted over my face.

"Did you tell her about school? About my hijab?" she whispered.

I couldn't lie; she'd see it in my face. "Not on purpose. You were in one of the photos."

"Is she going to tell my parents?"

"She said she wouldn't. She thinks you should tell them."

Mariam dropped the pin in her hand and huffed. "As if." She took a big breath. "They'd be furious. I'd get in so much trouble."

And the party she wanted to go to tonight? Had she thought about what her parents would do if they found out? "Is it really worth it?"

She looked at me as if I'd never understand, like I was a five-year-old and she was trying to explain quantum mechanics to me. "I want to be both. Canadian and a Muslim. But my parents, they think it can only be one way."

"I'm both. I play basketball, hang out with other kids, and you and Amira. Why do we have to choose?"

"You *think* you are, but are you? How much hanging out with other kids have you done lately? No one paid any attention to me until I took off my hijab. *Now* the boys look at me. They never did before." She let her shoulders slump and dropped the fabric to her lap. "I want to go to a party with Carmina tonight. *That's* why I asked if I could come over. My parents would never have said yes. I was going to sneak out and meet her and then come back to your house after. I was going to ask you to cover for me." She looked at me with something between resentment and apology, as if she was angry she had to tell me and sorry about it at the same time.

I raised my eyebrows, pretending to be shocked by the news. "You were?"

"Yeah." She sighed. "But now that I'm here … I don't think I can go through with it."

I should have felt triumphant that she didn't want to go to the party. But as I watched her glum face, I felt bad for her. She was caught between the life she had and the life she wanted, or thought she wanted. Her phone buzzed with a text. "Carmina," she said, checking it. "She's wondering what time I'll get there." She studied the half-done head covering and frowned, then turned back to her phone. Her fingers flew over the keys as she sent a response.

"What did you say?" I asked. *If she goes, I won't be mad at her,* I promised myself. At least she'd been honest about it.

Her mouth twitched. "That something came up and I can't make it." Mariam put her phone down on my bed. "We should go eat."

My stomach twisted. Things had turned out how I wanted: Mariam was hanging out with me, just like she used to. But it was bittersweet, like I'd won a prize by cheating. I didn't want my friend to be sad, feeling like she was missing out on something. And, I didn't want to be the runner-up to what she really wanted to be doing.

"You should go to the party." Even though I'd been thinking them, hearing the words actually come out of my mouth surprised me. Mariam stared at me like she hadn't heard right. "I'm serious. I'll cover for you," I added.

Mariam drew her eyebrows together and then fell back on my bed and stared at the ceiling. "I'm so confused!"

"Sometimes, when I'm at basketball, I want to take my hijab off so badly. It's hot and I hate not being able to see because the scarf gets in my way. I don't though. I just know it's not me. I feel like if I take it off once, what will stop me from taking if off other days, too?"

Mariam propped herself up on her elbows. "The first time I took off my head covering, I was so nervous. My hands were shaking. I thought I was going to be struck down by lightning. And then, it got easier. I liked being someone else at school."

"It's not who you are."

"It's not who I was." Mariam swallowed. She fingered the fringe on the scarf around her neck. "I don't know if I can go back to wearing it. My clothes, too. I like looking like the other girls."

She looked like me when she was in her hijab. And Amira. Didn't we count? "Are you worried Josh won't like you if you look Muslim?"

Mariam turned away. She didn't have to say anything, the answer was clear on her face.

"If he really liked you, it wouldn't matter what you're wearing."

She gave a long sigh and shook her head. "I don't really like him," she whispered. "I just picked him to be like the other girls."

"Oh, Mariam." I sat beside her on the bed and tucked my hands between my knees.

"He likes you, anyway."

"He doesn't —" I started to argue but she silenced me with a look.

"He does. I've seen him watching you at practice. I'm a horrible friend," she said quietly.

"No, you're not." I looked at the patterns on the floor and her sketch. She was confused and trying to figure out who she was, but she was far from a horrible friend.

CHAPTER 16

Mariam had been texting me all weekend with updates on the uniform. She'd worked on it all day Sunday and said it would be done for Monday morning. I'd have to try it on at school so she could see what areas needed to be fixed.

I was also anxious to find out if anything else had changed. Would she be wearing her hijab? Or would the pressure to look like other girls win out?

"*Marhaba*," I greeted Amira as she walked past me in the hallway. Her backpack dangled from her arm like a dead thing. "Amira?" She ignored me and kept walking to her locker, a few down from mine. I followed her, confused. "What's the matter?"

She kept her mouth in a firm line and stuffed her backpack inside her locker, letting it clang shut. "I want to go home."

Homesickness. A reasonable emotion, I thought to myself. To be honest, I was surprised she hadn't reacted this way earlier. She'd arrived during a cold snap. News reports lamented the frigid temperatures. Dad had let the car run for ten minutes to warm it up this morning before he drove me to school.

"I. Want. To. Go. Home!" This time the words came out angrier. She glared at me and I took a step back. The timid girl from last week had disappeared over the weekend.

"Amira —" I kept my voice hushed. I didn't want her to draw attention to herself, or me. "This is your home now."

"This is not my home," she spat. "We had nowhere else to go!"

No one around us understood Arabic, but they'd know she was mad about something. I grabbed her elbow to lead her to the washroom, but she shook me off, wrenching her sleeve from my grip. "Don't touch me. I don't want to go anywhere with you."

"Fine," I whispered back at her. "I was just trying to help."

"I don't need your help!" Amira pushed past me and bolted for the classroom.

"What was that about?" Mariam asked. She had the bag with the uniform in her hands.

"She's homesick," I said shaking my head.

"I thought you said she'd lived in a refugee camp before coming here."

"She did."

Mariam snorted in disbelief. "How could she miss *that*?" Mariam had left Egypt, but not as a refugee either. Her family had chosen to leave after the Arab Spring movement began. With family spread out around the world, they'd have been willing to go anywhere, but Canada had accepted them first. Mariam used to Facetime her friends sometimes, which was tricky with the time change. Over the years, her connection to them had dwindled. I wondered what they would think if they knew she was de-jabbing every morning at school.

"Must be hard, coming with nothing," I said. "It was sad about her friends, how she doesn't know where they are. And her family is scattered all over. Some of them are still in Lebanon." I felt a twinge of annoyance that I had to explain all this to her. "I think she needs some friends," I gave Mariam a meaningful look. "Even if she doesn't act like it."

Mariam narrowed her eyes at me. "What's that supposed to mean?"

"If you feel so bad for her, you could talk to her or sit with her at lunch or something."

"I *do* talk to her," Mariam fired back.

"Not just hi, but the way I do —"

"Because you're so perfect." The seething tone in her voice was like ice water.

"I didn't say I was perfect."

"You don't have to. I can see it when you look at me when I take off my scarf, like you're better than me. You're so judgmental!"

"I am not! But even if I am, at least I'm not two-faced. Coming to my house, hanging out with me, and then acting like *this* at school!"

Mariam glared at me, dropped the bag at my feet, and turned on her heel, stomping off without saying another word. Inside, I groaned. I'd said too much. I should have kept quiet. And just when things were getting better between us. Some Monday morning this was turning out to be. With an exasperated sigh, I picked up the bag and pulled out a corner of fabric. I didn't have the heart to try on the uniform, not without Mariam. Instead, I put the bag into my locker and hoped the argument would blow over by lunchtime.

"Hey, Sadia!" Josh called out, grinning

"Hi." I gave him a lacklustre greeting and watched him out of the corner of my eye as he walked to class. I sighed to myself, thinking about Amira and my argument with Mariam and how hard it would be to explain things about my family to someone like Josh.

Miss McKay took Amira out of the classroom to work on her English before I even sat down. I wished I could have gone with her, instead of dealing with Mariam's icy silence. Once again, she sat beside me, bare-headed. I wondered if she'd intended to, or if our argument had pushed her to do it. "O Canada" hadn't started yet, and I caught snippets of her conversation with Carmina as we waited for it to begin. "It was so fun! Daniel talked to me! We had, like, a real conversation! But guess what?" She looked over her shoulder toward the back of the class. "I spent most of the party with *Riley*!"

Mariam gaped. "Riley Penner?"

"He's really funny once you get to know him. And super artistic. He showed me pictures of some of the things he's drawn."

Despite a bad start to the morning, I was happy for Carmina. Riley was a nice guy, and if liking him meant I never had to hear the name Daniel again, I was all for it.

"Josh was there." Carmina singsonged the last bit, tempting Mariam.

"He was!" Mariam squealed, darting a quick look his way. *Fake,* I thought. *Imposter.* "Yeah! *Everybody* was there." I watched as Mariam's smile faded. Carmina's words had hit a sore spot.

"Like I told you, it just didn't work. I tried to get out —"

Part of me wanted to stand on my desk and shout, "LIAR!" at the top of my lungs. I sat fuming, clenching a pen in my hand so hard I thought I might break it. I had to say something, I couldn't keep quiet any longer.

"Did you tell Carmina about the uniform?" I asked, leaning over toward them.

Mariam gave me a warning look, but I ignored it and kept talking.

"Mariam came over Saturday and then worked on it all weekend."

"Oh," Carmina said, surprised.

Mariam's eyes flashed angrily at me. "Yeah, my parents *made* me go to Sadia's."

Carmina looked between us, confused by the glares we were shooting at each other.

I so badly wanted to tell Carmina that Mariam's parents had had nothing to do with her decision to stay at my house and ditch the party. As I opened my mouth to say something, Amira walked in. Her eyes were puffy and red.

"Amira?" I asked, leaning over. "Are you okay?" I spoke quietly in Arabic and looked over at Mariam. The expression on her face shifted from anger to concern. Our argument fizzled out. "Amira?"

She didn't answer me, so I left her alone. I didn't know what else to do to help her, or if help was even what she wanted.

At the end of class, I leaned toward Mariam. "I'm going to try on my uniform at today's practice," I told her quietly. It wasn't an apology, but at least it told her I wasn't holding a grudge.

I didn't know if I'd get a reply. Part of me expected her to ignore me, but I wasn't willing to walk away from three years of friendship.

I saw her glance at Amira. "I'll be there," she said.

When I got to the cafeteria for lunch, there was no space at Mariam and Carmina's table. *Of course,* I grumbled to myself. I scanned the room and found Amira sitting apart from a group of older kids at a table by the door. "Hi!" I said and sat down beside her.

She looked surprised to see me, and shifted over so I could join her. "I'm sorry about this morning," she mumbled.

"It's okay. I remember what it was like. The culture shock part, anyway."

She let out a long sigh. "Culture shock? Is that what this is?" She looked at me woefully. "My parents keep telling me to be grateful. And I am. It's just —"

"It's lonely," I said.

She nodded quickly and blinked away some tears.

"Do you want to come to basketball practice with me today? Mr. Letner wouldn't mind. You could watch or take shots. If you do come, you can see the uniform Mariam sewed for me. It's hijab, but I can play in it. No more head scarf flying all over the place." She gave a hesitant nod. It would have been hard to leave her by herself in the cafeteria and go to the gym.

"I can't believe your parents allow you to play," she said.

I shrugged. "They know how much I love it. Plus, the co-ed team only plays in one tournament. Hopefully, I'll make the JV girls team."

Mariam walked toward our table. I thought she'd ignore me, but I was wrong. "Can I sit here?" she asked in Arabic. Amira and I squished over to make room for her. "I was thinking ..." She looked at Amira. "I could use some help managing the team."

Amira looked up at her in surprise. "What could I do?"

Mariam shrugged. "We'll think of something." Amid all the chatter and chair scraping of the cafeteria, I met Mariam's eyes and gave her a grateful smile.

"I *do* remember how hard it was when we moved here," Mariam said to me under her breath. "I'm glad I don't have to do it over again."

"We were lucky. We had each other." I thought about Mr. Letner's photography assignment and how the perspective I'd had as a newcomer had shifted the longer I lived in Canada. Over time, Amira's would to; she'd think of Canada as her home. Syria, her lost friends, and everything she'd gone through would dull into dim memories. But right now, their loss was sharp and painful, like walking across broken glass. I wished there was something I could do to help her through it.

I held my breath as I wiggled into the uniform in a stall in the girls' change room. I put on the shirt first, long-sleeved and dark blue. The fabric was featherlight. The pants were slim but not tight and tapered at the ankles so they let me move comfortably. There were little mistakes in her sewing: fabric had been caught into the stitches or a hem was crooked, but from a distance, no one would be able to see that. Lastly, she put on the head covering. It felt comfortable, like a hood. The cap fit close to my head and she'd attached a looser piece of fabric under my chin so it draped like a scarf, but was secured on either side with snaps. I came out of the stall, walked past Amira and Mariam, and looked in the mirror. I liked what I saw: a girl ready to play basketball.

I spun past invisible guards and leaped across the change room to test its flexibility. I took a jump shot, raising my hands high in the air. I shook my head, trying to dislodge the head covering, but it stayed put.

"What do you think?" Mariam asked nervously. Amira stood beside her, a mixture of surprise and curiosity on her face.

I looked at Mariam with bright eyes. "It's perfect!" I proclaimed. "Perfect!"

Mariam beamed at me. "It was so hard to get the neckline right. I ripped it out like five times." She fingered the edges of the shirt. "There are some mistakes, but it was my first one. I think I could make it better if I —"

I cut her off. "Mariam, it's perfect!"

She grinned. "Okay. Good."

Practice was starting in a few minutes and the other girls on the team filtered into the change room. Each one of them stared at my new outfit, wide-eyed. They couldn't believe Mariam had made it.

"Maybe you should make one for all of us," Jillian teased. "It can be our team uniform."

Mariam blushed, tucking her hair behind her ear, but I could tell she was pleased. The outfit was so comfortable, it reminded me of how I used to move when I was a kid. There was nothing hampering me. I felt like I could do a slam dunk.

"Wow. Mariam's a really good friend," Jillian said when Mariam and Amira had left the change room. "You're lucky."

I thought about all the ups and downs we'd had lately. Sewing the uniform must have taken Mariam hours. But she'd done it for me. As I ran my hands over the snug-fitting headpiece, I knew I wouldn't miss an elbow flying toward my nose again. "Yeah, I am lucky," I agreed.

When I came out of the change room, Mariam and Amira were sitting on the bench by the gym office. Mariam was explaining something to her in Arabic. I took a ball from the bin and jogged over to a hoop to take shots beside Allan. For a second, I got nervous. What if he made fun of it? I swallowed back my nerves and aimed at the hoop. He did a double take at what I was wearing. "You look like a basketball ninja," he said quietly.

I gave a laugh of surprise. "Thanks." *I think.* My shot bounced off the backboard and went in.

I turned to the gym bench. Mariam hadn't heard Allan's comment, but I gave her a thumbs-up. She gave me an excited grin. There was a row of folded jerseys on the bench beside her. "If you want your jersey, come on over," she called to the team. She had a paper with our names and jersey numbers. Amira was in charge of making sure each person got the right jersey. "Here's number seven," Mariam said and handed me my jersey. She'd sewn a band across the bottom so it was longer than the others and hit mid-thigh.

I held up Kyle Lowry's number.

"Put it on. I want to see how the whole thing looks together," Mariam said to me.

Just as I slipped it over my head, Mr. Letner walked out of the gym office, chewing a half-eaten apple. "Did you make that?" he asked Mariam. He looked stunned.

"I never thought —" he broke off, looking between the two of us.

"Anyone bring their camera today?" Mr. Letner asked. "Mariam?"

She shook her head. "I left it at home."

"Mine's in my locker," I offered.

"Go grab it," Mr. Letner said. "We'll start practice when you get back." I dashed away, enjoying the sensation of running in my new uniform.

When I got back, I handed Mr. Letner my camera, but he was still eating his apple. He nodded at Josh. "You take the photo, Josh. I want both girls in it."

"Wait!" Mariam said. "I'll be right back." She darted into the change room. *To fix your hair?* I wondered.

When Mariam came back, she was in hijab; her shirt was long and dark denim and she had a grey head scarf hanging loose, but made with the same fabric as my uniform. "I'm in team colours," she said. "Okay, now I'm ready!" She put her arm around my shoulders and the other hand on her hip. I held a basketball against my side and tilted my head toward her. The two of us grinned at Josh, who held the camera up to his face. "Say, one, two, three, Thunder!"

"One, two, three, Thunder!" we repeated and he took the photo, bringing the camera around to show us the shot on the viewing screen. I liked what I saw. The two of us, side by side, like a team.

"Now *that* is a passion project!" Mr. Letner beamed at Mariam. "You solved a problem using creativity and talent. I'm really proud of you."

Mariam blushed at his compliments.

"Want me to take some action shots of you?" Josh asked me.

Mariam moved to stand by his side as he held up the camera. I dribbled the ball upcourt and leaped. The ball arced and went down in the basket. It was as close to a slam dunk as I could get.

CHAPTER 17

Amira's lips moved as she silently read the word Mr. Letner had written on the board. After being at school for only a few weeks, she was already getting better at reading English, even if she couldn't understand what all the words meant.

I translated it into Arabic for her. "It's another photography term." But there was another reason he had picked *Focus*. The tournament was this weekend, and between our photographs going up at the gallery soon and the passion projects, we'd all had a lot going on.

It was Allan's turn to do the Friday announcements from the office. I had a feeling Mrs. Mooney was leaning over his shoulder, making sure he followed the script. Once "O Canada" finished, his voice boomed out and we cringed at the volume.

After he'd gotten through the usual announcements of daily activities, including a reminder that Monday was a day off — for the kids anyway, because the teachers had meetings — he put on his best sports announcer voice and said, "And here's a special announcement from Mariam Hassanin, team manager for the JV All-City Tournament basketball team."

I'd thought she was in the washroom taking off her hijab and was surprised to hear her voice come through the speakers. "The co-ed tournament is this weekend at the Riverview Sportsplex. The JV team's first game is at nine o'clock. Come out to cheer on the Thunder!" I'd never heard Mariam on the announcements before. Her voice sounded soft and whispery.

"That's tomorrow, people!" Allan said, still struggling with volume. He must have been holding the microphone right up to his lips, like a rapper, because his voice was thick with static. "Come out to cheer us on. Or else!"

Everyone in our class laughed as the speakers clicked off. "What did he say?" Amira asked me.

"He told everyone they better come to watch our basketball game." It was hard to keep the excitement out of my voice.

"I wish I could go," she said with a sigh. "I don't know how to get there."

The sportsplex was across the city. Without a car, it would be a long and complicated bus ride. "It's pretty far, actually."

Miss McKay showed up at our classroom door and beckoned for Amira to join her. She stood up and waved goodbye to me just as Mariam and Allan came back into the class. "Good job!" I wrote on the margin of my notes and turned my scribbler to Mariam so she could read it. She gave me a grateful smile. "I was so nervous!" she mouthed.

Mariam hadn't had time to take off her hijab before announcements. Seeing her in it made me feel like things were back to normal between us, at least for now.

Mr. Letner stood at the front of the room and waited for everyone to hand in yesterday's reading response. "We're going to do some work on your photographs this class. The art show is coming up quick, so if you haven't already decided which picture you'd like to display, today is the day to do it! I also need a write-up for the photo. Remember, it will be open to the public, so choose accordingly." He gave Allan a pointed look.

Allan held his hands out in an innocent, "why me?" look. The truth was we'd all been seeing a different side of Allan. Since that first photo of him and his brother Cody, Allan had given us other glimpses into what it was like living with a physically challenged person. Cody was always smiling in the photos, except for the one of him doing physiotherapy. In it, his face had been contorted in pain as he did an exercise. "It's to keep his muscles working," Allan had said. "Sometimes it hurts so bad that he cries, but the next day, he does it again. He has to."

"Before we go to the lab to work on the photos, I want to talk about the F-word on the board." There was a round of laughter. "*Focus.* Make sure the photo you choose isn't just in focus, but *has* a focus." He looked at all of us for a long minute, making sure his words sunk in.

We traipsed down to the computer lab, cameras in tow. I still hadn't downloaded the photo of Mariam and me from when I'd tried on my uniform for the first time. It was special to me, but compared to what other people were choosing, not artsy enough for the divisional art show. I looked through my file of saved photos. Most of them were basketball related. My favourite was still the one Josh had taken of me in hijab, holding the basketball. It wasn't artsy either, but it broke down stereotypes about Muslim girls. I opened up a Word document and started typing a title for the photo. "If you give a girl a basketball …"

Amira returned from her class with Miss McKay and slid into the spot next to me. "Guess what?" she asked. Her eyes crinkled in the corners as she smiled.

"What?"

"Miss McKay is taking me to the tournament! We called my parents and they agreed. I'll get to watch your first game on Saturday."

"That's great!" I gushed. I remembered sitting in the stands watching Aazim play basketball when we'd first moved here. I'd prayed for a week that Aazim's team would win the tournament. I thought the kids looked like giants. They lost in the quarter-finals, but I couldn't get the smell of the waxed gym floors and squeaking rubber shoes out of my mind. *One day, I'll play in the tournament,* I'd promised myself. And now, a few years later, I was.

My eyes drifted across to Amira's screen. She'd taken pictures at her apartment. Seven people crammed around a kitchen table piled high with plates of food. There weren't enough chairs for everyone, so the little kids sat on the counter. Next photo: the kids' room. There were bunk beds for her brothers and a single bed for Amira pushed against the wall, with a curtain strung up for privacy. Clothes for all the kids lay in tidy piles on the floor. It was hard to imagine that five kids could share one room, but they didn't have a choice.

The next shot was a close-up of a medal. Glinting golden, it hung off the post of her bed on a red ribbon. I could make out the words on it: "First Place 100 Metres" and the date of last year's divisional track meet. I gave a quick gasp of surprise. I knew who had won that medal. Across the room, Josh sat at his computer, head bent, neck craned over the keyboard. Josh had won three running events last year, and we'd all cheered for him. The boys had called it a "hat trick" and thrown their baseball caps at him when he'd won the final event. I didn't know what *hat trick* meant and was too worried I wouldn't get my Raptors hat back to throw it on the field. I sat back in my chair, incredulous. Josh had given Amira one of his medals to replace the one she'd left behind in Syria.

Amira had already switched to a new photo. This one was her little brother. He looked about five years old. He was on a toboggan, snow on the hill around him, towering pine trees behind. The smile on his face stretched from cheek to cheek; his eyes were bright. I couldn't resist laughing. I remembered the first time I'd flown down a hill, riding the snow and landing in a heap at the bottom. "He looks happy," I said.

Amira looked at me, a wistful smile on her face, too.

"He is." There was such weight to her words, like she was a parent looking at her child's photograph. He was young and wouldn't remember the hardship the family had endured; not like Amira.

"Did you go tobogganing?" I asked, pointing at the photo.

She hesitated, then shook her head. "I was scared."

I leaned in close to her. "I could show you how," I offered. "We could go to my house after school and I'll take you to a hill nearby."

She pressed her lips together. "I have to pick up my brothers and walk them home after school. I don't know where you live. How would I find your house?"

"I'll come with you," I suggested. "Then we can walk to the hill together."

I thought she'd jump at the chance, but she gave me a guarded look. "You don't have to."

"I want to," I told her.

"Girls," Mr. Letner's head poked up from a few rows ahead of us, twisting around to see who was talking. "Get to work."

I gave Amira a nudge. "We'll walk home together and then go sledding," I whispered with finality. She sighed and slowly nodded her head.

"Hey, Sadia!" Jillian called as she stuffed her gym clothes into her bag after practice. It took me longer to change out of my uniform than the other girls and I was usually the last one out.

"Since there's no school on Monday, my sister is having a party on Sunday night. I told her I'd keep quiet about it if I got to invite some friends." She gave me a conspiratorial smirk. "My parents are going skiing for a couple of days."

Jillian's sister was in grade eleven. She looked like Jillian, blond and athletic. She ate lunch in the cafeteria with a group of grade twelve students, and even though Jillian didn't say anything, I knew a party her sister threw wouldn't be an innocent movie night.

I hesitated before answering. I should have said no for all the reasons my parents would want me to: there'd be drinking, boys, and no parents. Not a good combination for a Muslim girl.

But the offer was tantalizing. And then Jillian said, "Josh asked me to make sure you were invited."

"He did?"

She nodded her head excitedly. "Yeah. I mean, I'm inviting the whole team, but he specifically asked about you."

My stomach fluttered and I bit back a smile. How could I not go? "The *whole* team? Even Mariam?"

"I was sort of thinking players only." She looked apologetic. "But I guess it makes it awkward for you if I don't invite her."

"Yeah, kind of. She'll be at the tournament," I pointed out.

Jillian shrugged. "True. Yeah, let her know." Jillian's ponytail swung behind her as she left the change room.

After practising with the team over lunch hours and mornings for the last few weeks, we'd gotten close. Most days, we all sat together in the cafeteria; Josh usually found a way to sit across or beside me and we'd get into heated discussions about whose favourite team was better, the Raptors or his Golden State Warriors.

I knew nothing could happen between us. Dating and boyfriends were completely off-limits for me. But it was getting harder and harder to ignore how much I liked being around him.

I settled in to Math class and pulled my phone out of my pocket. The teacher was writing the answers for yesterday's homework on the board. I quickly sent Mariam a text. *Jillian invited us to her sister's party.*

A got a response seconds later. A giggling, blushing emoji. *When?*

Sunday night. Whole team is invited. Her parents are out of town.

Mariam didn't wait for a reply before she sent a follow-up text: *Don't tell your parents.* It was accompanied by a blushing emoji holding a finger to its lips.

The truth was, my parents wouldn't stop me from going to a party with my team, even if the guys were there. Mariam's parents would. But if my mom and dad knew what the party was *really* going to be like, it would be a definite no. If Mariam and I wanted to go, we would have to be creative. I thought back to when she'd tried to use me as a cover to go to the party at Carmina's. Funny how a few weeks ago, I'd judged her for doing it, and now I was tempted to do the same thing.

It was last period English with Mr. Letner. I'd changed into my basketball uniform to help Mariam present our passion project.

Mr. Letner stood at the front of the class. Even though only some of us were doing a passion project, Mr. Letner wanted us to present them so everyone could see what we'd been working on. "I asked Mariam to go first because she embodies everything a passion project is supposed to be." He moved to the side of the classroom as Mariam and I came to the front. "She used her talent to do something that improved someone's life. Am I right on that, Sadia?"

I nodded and then frowned at Mr. Letner. This was *Mariam's* passion project? I thought it was mine, too. Somewhere along the way, I'd figured designing and sewing a new uniform was also my passion project. But as I listened to Mariam, I realized how much thought and skill had gone into making it. She'd thought of everything down to using something called a serger to make seams that didn't rub against my skin. I stood mute while she explained what she had made and why. She'd brought in the pattern pieces she'd used and all her supplies, as well as some other things she'd made, like clothes for herself. She had me do a couple of fake basketball moves to demonstrate how much easier it was to move in the outfit she'd sewed for me.

Mariam flushed with pride and did a little bow at the end of her presentation. Everyone clapped. "Any questions?" she asked.

Avery's hand went up. "What about other Muslim girls who play sports? What do they wear?"

"Just their normal clothes, I guess."

"You should start a clothing line."

Mariam lifted one shoulder in a shrug. "I never thought of that."

"You could call it Re-jab!" Allan shouted out. "Get it? Re-jab? Like *hi*jab, but *re*designed?"

Mariam gave a surprised laugh. Who would have though Allan would come up with such a good name?

Mr. Letner nodded. "There are probably other girls like Sadia who want to play sports but can't because the hijab moves around or gets in the way. Anyone want to design the website? Start a marketing campaign? That could be *your* passion project: to see what it takes to get a business off the ground." Larissa and Christian looked at each other and put their hands up. "Okay." Mr. Letner pointed at them with the rolled-up paper in his hand. "There you go, Mariam. You've got a marketing team." I thought of the other girls at the mosque. Maybe they didn't play sports because of the problems wearing hijab posed. If other girls saw that I could do it, then maybe they would, too.

CHAPTER 18

It had been a long time since I'd been tobogganing. But taking Amira was more fun than I'd thought it would be. Taking her three little brothers home from school was not. They didn't stop talking. They ran ahead and didn't listen when she called for them to stop. One, Yussef, found a stick and started to poke the other two with it. The Amira who sat passively at school all day was nothing like the bossy, bustling big sister who walked home with me and the boys. When one of them climbed a snowbank too close to the street, she yanked him off and reamed him out so loudly the other two ran for cover. "Brothers," Amira said with an eye roll when she let him go. I gave her a sympathetic smile, even though Aazim had never been the rough-and-tumble sort.

We walked half a block without saying anything. It wasn't awkward; it was kind of nice, actually. She looked at me pensively, frowning, like she was trying to decide if she should say something. "What?" I prompted.

"Do you like it here?" she asked.

"Where? In Canada? Or in this neighbourhood?"

"Both, I guess."

"It's different than Syria, that's for sure, but I was younger when I moved here. I was about his age." I nodded at Omar. He was the second oldest and went to my old middle school.

"I thought it would be easier," she confessed.

Dad had prepared us, telling us about his life in the U.K., before we'd moved to Canada. He'd made it sound like a fairy-tale world, which was my dad's way; he loved to embellish and put energy into telling a story and keeping his audience glued to him. We'd been excited to arrive and see this wonderful new place. It was different for Amira. She'd been homeless, living in a camp for a year and a half. I thought of everything that she'd told me about leaving her friends and what life had been like once the war started. Leaving Syria the way she had must still twist her up inside.

"That's our apartment building," she said and pointed to a four-storey building across the street. She corralled her brothers, hooking her fingers into the jacket collars of the two youngest and guiding them to the other side. "I can wait out here," I said when we reached the front steps. The days were short at this time of year, so even though it was only four o'clock, the sun sat low in the sky. Her building was on a busy street without any trees. I could tell which apartment was hers because her mother had hung blankets and quilts over the balcony railing to air them out.

"No, you better come in. My parents will have questions for you. Also, we should pray *Asr* before we go, don't you think?" She was right. I usually did my late afternoon prayers when I got home from school, but by the time we finished tobogganing, the sun would have set.

We trudged up the stairs, our boots leaving wet footprints as the snow melted off them. The boys' cheeks were rosy, more from running than the cold. Mariam's dad was waiting at the top of the stairs and patted each boy on the head as they ran past him to the open door. "This is Sadia," Amira said.

"*Marhaba*," I said.

"I remember you. You showed Amira around on her first day."

I nodded.

"She wants to take me tobogganing," Amira said.

He hesitated. I knew that look, I'd seen it on my parents' faces lots of time. He was wondering if it was safe.

"I'll walk her home after," I suggested with a smile. Mr. Nasser frowned, considering his options. "And I can give you my cell number, in case you need to get ahold of us."

Mr. Nasser agreed to that. He pulled an older iPhone out of his pocket, probably the only form of communication the whole family had. I rattled off my number and he thumbed it in. "Come," he said, waving us toward the open door. "Amal will want to meet you."

Amira's mom sat on the couch with the youngest boy, who had just woken up from a nap. His eyes were glazed and he snuggled closer against her chest when I walked in. "Hi," I greeted her.

She smiled and nodded back at me. "You brought a friend?" she asked Amira.

"Yes, this is Sadia from school. You've met her before."

"Oh, yes! How could I have forgotten!" Mrs. Nasser lowered her voice. "You're the basketball player! Amira talks about you. You play in hijab, she said. With the boys!" Mrs. Nasser looked at me as if she couldn't believe it.

I looked around the apartment. It didn't take much for a family of seven to fill up a two-bedroom apartment. Besides a couch and a loveseat, a few donated toys were in bins against the wall, as well as a TV, and on a scuffed coffee table lay her parents' English workbooks.

The boys had moved to the kitchen, where they munched on a snack of cut-up apples and crackers. With only two short counters, I couldn't imagine how Mrs. Nasser cooked and fed all of them at once. Guiltily, I thought of my house and how large it was. We each had our own room and more TVs than people. Was this what my life would have been like if Mom and Dad had waited to leave Syria?

Mr. Nasser told Amira's mom what we wanted to do. As soon as she heard, she turned to the boys. "No," Amira said. "Please, can it just be us? I can take the boys later. Tomorrow maybe."

Mrs. Nasser looked at her, disappointed, but she nodded. "Yes, go. Have a good time."

I wondered if she'd forgotten about praying, but she took off her jacket and motioned for me to do the same. "We can wash and then pray in my parents' room." Part of me wanted to get outside before it got too dark, but I also knew prayers were important to Amira. At school she made her way to the room set aside for us every lunch hour. It was probably the one time of the school day when she could relax and focus on something familiar.

After we'd washed, Amira took me to her parents' room. Crowded with a bed, dresser, and crib, there was barely enough room for prayer mats on the floor. She closed the door so we could have privacy.

As I went through the motions of the *Asr* prayer, our voices mingling together, I thought about the tournament tomorrow and how much playing well would mean not just to me, but to my team, and even to Mariam and Amira.

When we were finished, we rolled up the prayer mats and Amira stowed them away in the corner.

"*Ma'a as-salama*," I called to her family as we left, dressed again in our outdoor clothes. They said goodbye as well, and one of Amira's little brothers ran to the door to give her a kiss and me a high-five.

"Where do you live?" she asked as we walked.

"Close to you, actually. If you take a left off this street, you'll see a sign for Beechwood Estates. That's our neighbourhood."

"You have a house?"

I nodded.

"We had a house in Homs. It was just outside the city centre. Neighbours we met in the camp told us it had been bombed. Nothing was left."

"Was anyone you knew —"

She nodded before I finished the question. I knew Homs had been hit hard from watching it on the news. I was reminded again how lucky I was that my parents had decided to leave when they had. "The hill is just there, on the other side of the community centre," I said to change the subject.

Two hockey rinks, already filled with kids, stood between us and the hill. "Do all Canadian kids learn to skate?" she asked.

"Lots, but maybe not all. Would you like to learn?"

She shook her head and moved closer to me. "No!"

I laughed. "It's hard! Dad took us out once, but never again. There's a bin of donated equipment inside the building, though, if your brothers wanted to try it." A couple of kids, younger than Yussef, flew around the rink. One wore a pink helmet, her blond hair flowing over her jacket.

Amira got quiet as she watched them. "Do you remember that day at school when I was so upset?" She gave me a shy glance. I'd chalked it up to homesickness, but the way she asked, I could tell it was more. "It was my best friend's fiteenth birthday."

"You still don't know where she is?" I asked.

She shook her head. "No one's heard from anyone in her family. I miss her so much. We never got to say goodbye."

"There's no way to find out where they went? Could your parents help?"

Amira shook her head. "Life is hard enough. I don't want to burden them with something else."

"But there must be a way to find them. I mean, all the people spread out over different continents. There has to be some way to track them. Aren't there any organizations that can help?"

Amira looked at me sideways. "If there are, I don't know about them." Her cheeks and nose glowed pink from the cold and her breath came out in smoky puffs. I let the matter drop, but it stuck in my head. Amira's friends might be in Canada, too, maybe even in the same city! What if they could be tracked down?

Amira started walking again and I followed. Thoughts of her friends must hang over her all the time. I couldn't imagine living with that stress. No wonder she looked haunted.

Our boots crunched across the snowy field toward the hill. "We can use those," I told Amira and pointed to a few shiny plastic toboggans sitting at the bottom of the hill. The initials of the community centre were written on them in black marker for people who didn't have their own.

We each grabbed one and trudged up to the top of the hill. Fresh snow started to fall, the flakes like dollops of cream; they stuck to our winter jackets and head scarves. Someone had created a jump partway down the hill by packing down snow in a mound. In all other directions, the toboggans and snowboards had carved out grooves — straight shots down the hill to the field below. "Want me to go first?" I asked, already straddling the sled.

I'd barely waited for her to say yes before I crossed my legs. I held the handle in one hand and pushed myself off with the other. The sunny day had left a crust of shiny, icy snow and the sled flew down the hill. I couldn't resist squealing as it fishtailed toward the bottom, finally spinning and flipping over. I landed in a heap, my scarf half off.

"Your turn!" I called, standing up and shaking off the snow. Amira stood at the top, but she didn't move. I waited for a minute. "Come on! It's fun!"

With a groan, I walked back up the hill, dragging my sled behind me. "Do you want me to go down with you?" I asked. Amira nodded.

"I don't want to fall off."

I didn't tell her that was half the fun; you kind of had to learn that on your own. "Come on," I said and sat at the front of the sled. "Get on." Amira clutched my shoulders, kneeling behind me. From up here, the expanse of the field stretched out below us. We weren't that high, but for a person who had never seen snow until a few weeks ago, I guess it was scary. As soon as I pushed off, Amira started shrieking. She didn't stop until we got to the bottom.

"So? Still think it's scary?"

"No!" she said. Laughter made her eyes crinkle. She waited until I was standing and then raced back up the hill.

We tobogganed for an hour. By the time I pulled off my mittens and checked the time on my phone, my tailbone ached and my fingers and toes were numb. My stomach hurt from laughing because every time Amira got close to the bottom, she'd raise her hands in the air like people do on roller coasters. She'd fly off the sled in a wipeout that would have made her brothers proud. I'd warned her to avoid the jump, and she'd screamed in terror the first time she realized she was heading straight for it. I'd watched from the top of the hill as she went up, caught air, and landed with a spine-shaking thud in the new snow. My stomach dropped watching it happen, but then I'd heard her shriek of joy and I knew she was okay. After that, she started aiming for the jump. The whole time we'd been tobogganing, new snow had been falling. It coated everything, the ground, the trees, and us, with sticky clumps. Before we'd moved to Canada, I'd never thought there were so many different types of snow. My favourite was the sparkly powder that fell in the night. It looked magical, falling like diamonds in the dark sky.

"Fun," Amira said in English as we started for home. She was smiling and looked like a different person. White flakes of snow stuck to her hijab and the ends of her eyelashes for a second before melting.

I agreed. "That *was* fun."

"I like snow," she said, bending down to grab a handful. More kids had arrived to skate and we could hear the slap of the puck against boards. The lights over the hockey rinks had come on and illuminated the falling flakes. It looked like a snow globe come to life.

Even though it was almost dinnertime, the air had warmed up since we'd been outside, and the snow was sticky enough to make a snowball. I mashed it between my hands and showed her. "Snowball."

"Snowball," she repeated. I tossed it at her. The snowball hit her jacket. "Snowball fight," I yelled and grabbed another handful. We ran home laughing and dodging each other's snowballs.

CHAPTER 19

"You're coming to my tournament tomorrow, right?" I asked Aazim at dinner. I knew Mom and Dad would be there, but Aazim hadn't mentioned if he was coming.

He furrowed his brow. "I have to study all weekend," he said. "I have a test on Monday."

I glared at him. He shovelled food into his mouth, which gave him an excuse not to look at me. "But you have to come!" I'd gone to all Aazim's games when he played in high school. I couldn't believe he'd miss mine.

"Aazim's school work is important," Dad piped up.

"You could come for one game," I pointed out.

"I'll try," he said, ignoring my angry scowl.

"All you do is study." I huffed.

"Sadia," Mom said with a warning tone. "Leave your brother."

I pushed away my plate, no longer hungry, fuming at the double standard. I'd gone to watch him play. Shouldn't he be expected to watch me? Dad's eyes flashed at me. "If you're done, you can be excused."

"Fine," I said and stomped away. Every team he'd been on, I'd watched him play. How many games did that add up to over the years? He couldn't come to one of mine? He spent all his time at the university, holed up in the library, studying. When he came home, it was to eat and then retreat to his room for more studying. I watched him walk around mumbling to himself, so caught up in what he was thinking about that he ignored me. It was like university had stolen my brother from me.

There was a knock on my door. "Sadia?" Aazim called. "Can I come in?"

At first I was going to say no. I was too angry to speak to him. But what was the point in turning him away if he'd come to apologize? Maybe he'd come to my game after all. "Yes," I said in a wounded tone. I wanted to make sure he knew how hurt I was.

Aazim shut the door softly after him. We had the same eyes, but Aazim had Dad's nose, prominent with a bump in the middle. He had Dad's thick head of hair, too, and bushy eyebrows. I know girls thought he was handsome; I'd seen them watching him with interest at the mosque. Even Mariam had made comments about his looks, which made me pretend to gag.

"I need to tell you something, but you have to promise to keep it a secret from Mom and Dad."

I sat up straighter, curious.

"Studying isn't the real reason I can't come on the weekend. I don't have a test on Monday." Aazim took a deep breath. "I'm in a play."

I stared at him, stunned. My mouth might even have dropped open. "A play?"

He nodded. "At the theatre at university. Our first

show is tomorrow night. We have dress rehearsal during the day."

"Aazim!"

"I know," he said and sat down on the end of my bed, holding his head in his hands. "I know."

"When are you going to tell Mom and Dad?"

He lifted his head. "I'm not."

"You have to. They'd want to see you."

He scoffed and raised an eyebrow. "Really?"

"As long as you get into med school, they won't care what you do."

He set his mouth in a grim line. "That's the other thing."

"Oh no," I groaned.

"I dropped a couple of classes. It was too much to study and do the play. They were just three credit courses and I can take them in the summer." He shifted toward me and looked at me with pleading eyes. "I really love it. Being on stage, working with the other actors. We're good, Sadia! The director is from Toronto. He's here teaching a course and this is the only play he's directing. He picked me over all the theatre students to be one of the leads."

"You're a main character?"

He nodded.

"So all this time I thought you were studying, you were actually rehearsing?"

"Just since January. I saw the audition poster and thought, why not? What did I have to lose? I'd always wanted to try it. A friend of mine is in the backstage crew and convinced me to try out."

I stared at him, incredulous. My brother, on stage. I couldn't imagine it. "Tell me a line. Something you say in the play."

He stood up, cleared his throat, and recited a few lines. It wasn't long enough to understand the play, but his voice rang clear and strong, filled with emotion. Half of the stories Dad told were like well-acted plays. If Aazim had theatrical talent, he came by it honestly.

"Oh, boy." I sighed, falling back against my pillow.

"I'm sorry I can't be at the tournament," he said. "I really am."

"I wish I could see your play."

"Me, too." He sighed.

"How long does it run for? Maybe I could come with you to another show. We could tell Mom and Dad you're taking me to a basketball game at the university for some brother-sister bonding."

Aazim shook his head. "It's bad enough that I'm lying to them. I don't want to drag you into it, too."

"You should have us there, your family. At least me, if not Mom and Dad." I watched him mull it over. "You should tell them. They might surprise you."

He let out a long sigh. "I'd rather keep it a secret than go against them. Promise me you won't say anything."

I nodded. As much as I hated keeping the secret from Mom and Dad, I couldn't betray Aazim.

"I really love it," he admitted as he stood to go. "I feel a lot better now that I told you," he said. "I wish I'd done it weeks ago."

"Can I tell *you* a secret?" I asked him. He nodded and sat back down.

"There's this guy …" I let my words drift off.

Aazim's eyebrows shot up. "Uh-huh?"

"He's not Muslim."

Aazim gave a laugh of surprise. I slapped his leg. "Don't laugh! What should I do? He likes me, at least I think he does. And I think I might like him. And there's a party this weekend…." I let my voice trail off woefully.

He held up his hands in surrender. "Oh no, do *not* get me involved in that one. Me being in a play is one thing; I'm eighteen."

I frowned at him. "I just need to know what to tell him. Should I say nothing? Let him figure it out? And what about the party? Older kids are going to be there and Jillian's parents are out of town." I groaned in frustration. "Why does everything have to be so difficult?"

Aazim patted my shoulder. "Mom and Dad might surprise you," he said, repeating my words back to me. I picked a stuffy up from the pile on my bed and tossed it at his head. He dodged it and laughed. "Let me know how it works out for you."

After he left, I flopped back down on my pillows, wishing that things could be as straightforward as a game of basketball.

CHAPTER 20

I'd woken up before my alarm went off that morning, excited for the tournament. But as we drove across town to the sportsplex, my excitement turned to nerves.

"You're quiet," Mom commented, turning in her seat to look at me. "Are you nervous?"

I nodded. There were so many things running through my head. I turned my attention to the brightening sky outside. I'd put on the uniform Mariam had made for me. At least I didn't have to worry about the outfit. It had proven itself during practices. I was excited for other teams to see it. Maybe they had female Muslim players who would want one, too. Mariam might actually be able to start her own business making them.

The parking lot was half full when we arrived. I spotted Mariam's family's car in the lot. As team manager, she'd wanted to arrive early like the rest of us. Our team had drawn the first game in our pool of six teams, which was good news because it gave us time to rest between each of the three games we'd play today. If we made the playoffs, there would be more games tomorrow.

My parents and I walked in together. Mr. Letner

was sitting with five other students on a bench against a wall in the front hallway: Josh and Allan, who'd probably come together, and Thomas, Jillian, and Mariam. Mariam's parents were standing nearby and waved when they saw us walk in. Mom and Dad went to talk to the Hassanins and I went to sit with my team. Mariam was in hijab because her parents were there.

As soon as Josh saw me, his face broke into a grin. "Hey, Sadia," he said and moved over so there was room for me between him and Jillian.

I bit back a smile and met his eyes, then looked away quick. The last thing I wanted was for Mom or Dad to notice. They couldn't stop me from liking him, but if they thought something was going on, it would lead to an awkward conversation about dating.

"Are your parents here?" I asked him. Lame question, but all of a sudden, I was nervous around him.

He scoffed. "My parents? No." He shook his head.

"Why not?"

"It's hockey season." He said it like that should explain everything.

I still didn't understand. He sighed and dropped his voice so only I could hear him. "It's my brother's draft year. Most weekends they go to watch him play. They're in Swift Current right now."

"Saskatchewan?" We'd driven through that town on our way to the Rockies last year. I didn't understand hockey the way other kids did. We didn't watch it on TV in my house, and neither Aazim nor I had ever played. But I'd seen the swagger that kids with team gear had and I could imagine being drafted was a big deal.

"Yeah. They left last night so I had to ask Mr. Letner for a ride," he confessed.

Josh looked at the dismay on my face and gave a little laugh, shaking his head. "It's okay, Sadia. They don't beat me or anything. It's just how my family is. Max is the priority right now."

He could shrug it off all he wanted, but I still felt a twinge of sadness for him. I liked knowing my parents were here to support me.

"There's a lot of kids from school here," he said looking around.

The turnout was surprising. More and more people kept streaming through the doors.

"They want to see us annihilate the competition," Allan said with narrow-eyed determination.

Mr. Letner gave him a warning look. "Let's just worry about playing like a team."

I grinned at Allan. For once, I had to agree with him: we *were* here to win.

Carmina walked in with a couple of other kids, including Riley, and ran over to wish us good luck. She unrolled the sign she'd made. It was a work of art, literally. "Go Thunder Go!" had been painted on it with graffiti-style lettering and the background was the school logo of Thor's hammer with a lightning bolt. "Riley and I worked on it all night."

"Wow!" I grinned at her. "That must have taken hours."

"It did," she singsonged happily.

Mr. Letner waited until the whole team had arrived and then sent everyone but me, because I was already in my uniform, to get changed in the locker rooms. I bent down to put on my basketball shoes while Mariam organized the player welcome bags, making sure there was one for each of us.

Mariam sat down beside me on the bench. She leaned in close and whispered in my ear. "I wish my mom and dad would leave. It feels like they're just staying to spy on me."

I lifted an eyebrow. "Spying? Really?"

She rolled her eyes and groaned. "That's what it feels like. They're going to be so bored. Neither of them likes basketball."

"At least my parents are here, too," I said. "They can keep them company."

"Did you say anything to your mom about Jillian's party?"

I shook my head. "Not yet. How about you?"

Mariam pressed her lips together and pulled her eyebrows in tight. "Here's what I'm thinking."

Oh no, I silently groaned. *I know that look.*

She leaned in close, an intense look on her face. "Ask your parents if I can sleep over. Even though it's a Sunday night, my parents will probably say yes because there's no school Monday. When we get to your house, we'll ask your mom if she can take us to the movie theatre at Forest Park Mall. I checked and there's a movie that starts at nine-thirty. Then we'll sneak out and walk to Jillian's house. We'll leave her house before eleven-thirty to get back to the movie theatre in time for your mom to pick us up."

Mariam was wasting her talent on sewing. She should be a military strategist. But as good as the plan sounded, all I could hear was the ring of warning bells in my head. "Mariam —"

She cut me off. "Please, Sadia! I missed the last party to hang out with you. Don't make me miss another one."

"You missed the last party because you wanted to, remember?"

"Whatever." She waved her hands like the details didn't matter. "You know what I mean. If we tell your parents we're going to Jillian's, they'll want to call my mom and make sure it's okay. What if they want to call Jillian's mom? They could wreck the party!"

I sighed, filled with indecision. "Let me think about it."

Mariam gave my uniform a pointed look, a reminder of all she'd done for me.

When the other kids were changed and ready, Mr. Letner stood up and gestured for us to follow him to the gym. I heard the kids from school before I saw them. Shouts and cheers from the bleachers filled the gym when we walked in and I almost felt bad for our opponents. Carmina stood on the top row, holding up her sign.

The sportsplex was so big that there was enough room for two courts on the gym floor. A curtain divided the spaces. Our team took their spots on the benches set up on one side, and the spectators sat on bleachers on the other side. A timekeeper was already at his table against the curtain and he was talking with the referee. The clock on the wall showed the countdown was on: fifteen minutes until game time.

We each grabbed a ball for warm-up, taking shots and running the same passing and driving drills that we used in practice. I gave my parents a thumbs-up as Mr. Letner called us in to go over our positions and last-minute pointers before the game began. "Excuse me, Coach?" The referee had walked over to our bench. An older man, he had greying hair that stuck out like wings over his ears. "Can I have a word?"

Mr. Letner looked annoyed, but put down his clipboard and stood up. "Sure."

Five minutes until game time.

The students in the bleachers had started chanting: "Let's go, Thunder, let's go!" My parents were clapping along with the beat of the words. Their voices were so loud the floor trembled. Over by the timekeeper's table, Mr. Letner was shaking his head and gesturing at us. His hands went to his hips and he stared down at the ref. "What's going on?" Josh asked, frowning. It wasn't like Mr. Letner to get so upset.

Mr. Letner marched across the gym floor and pulled a black binder out of his bag marked "Rule Book." He went back to the ref, flipping through the pages, stabbing his finger at something. He looked like he wanted to throw the binder at the ref, who continued to shake his head. "Oh, you've got to be kidding me!" Mr. Letner shouted. We all stared at him wide-eyed when he came back to the bench. His face was pulsing red. He took a moment to compose himself.

"Sadia, I need to speak to you." His voice was tight. Had I done something wrong?

The time clock was frozen at one minute to game time.

Mr. Letner led me away from the team. His mouth was pinched tight with anger. "I sent in a request to the officials when you first made the team, asking about your head scarf and if it would be a problem."

I nodded, remembering the conversation.

"I didn't hear back from them and assumed it was fine. Then when Mariam made you this new outfit, I felt confident that you'd be able to play."

A sick swell started in my stomach and rose up in my throat. I knew what was coming next and I didn't want to hear it. I wanted to close my ears so that Mr. Letner's words wouldn't echo in my brain. "The ref is telling me that your outfit doesn't comply with tournament rules and you can't play unless you change."

All I heard was:

Can't play.

Can't play.

Can't play.

I stood mute and gaped at my parents in the bleachers. One look at my face and Dad stood up. He held out his hand to help Mom step down the bleachers. Together, they walked across the court to where I was standing with Mr. Letner.

I barely heard him explain the problem. All I could think about was that I might not be able to play because of a stupid rule. Dad flapped his arms and said something about human rights. Mom pulled me against her and rubbed my shoulders. Mr. Letner shook his head in tight-lipped disbelief. When Dad demanded to see the rule book, Mr. Letner showed it to him and together they discussed the legality of it. "It's not just that," Mr. Letner said. "Part of the permission form you signed said you agreed with the terms and conditions of the league. There's no way around this, except for Sadia to take off her head covering."

Dad sputtered in outrage. "That's not possible."

"What should she do? Watch from the sidelines? She's been looking forward to this tournament all year!" Mom said, looking between them, eyebrows drawn together in anger.

Mr. Letner was at a loss. He looked helplessly at my parents.

"What's going on?" Mariam asked, coming to my side. "Is everything okay?" I turned to look at her. Tears welled in my eyes. From the gym entrance, I saw Amira enter with Miss McKay. She'd made it, come all this way to watch me play, for nothing.

"The official says Sadia's outfit is against regulations."

Mariam's face went from normal to volcanic in five seconds. Her eyes narrowed and her chin jutted forward. "That's not fair! Her outfit is totally regulation." I'd never seen Mariam so mad. She turned on her heel and was about to storm over to the ref when Mr. Letner put out his arm to bar her from going further.

"Arguing with him won't help."

The crowd in the bleachers was getting restless. They wanted the game to start or to find out what the holdup was. Josh stood up at the bench and held up his hands. "What's going on?" he shouted.

"They aren't letting Sadia play!" Mariam shouted back. I cringed and wished I could crawl under the bench. Now the whole gym knew. I'd never been embarrassed about my religion before. And I still wasn't. I wasn't embarrassed to *be* Muslim, but it was humiliating to be treated differently *because* I was Muslim.

"What?" The whole team stood in an uproar. "Why not?" "How come?" "Come on, Ref!" they all shouted.

The kids in the bleachers figured out what was going on.

"Come on!" Allan shouted. "Let her play! Let her play!" He raised his fist with each word and the team started to chant along.

Then, the people in the bleachers started. "Let her play!" they yelled in unison, stomping their feet to the beat. The ref from the other game came to ask everyone to quiet down, but that just made them cheer louder. Mariam started to chant it, too, and raised her arms to make the volume in the gym go up even higher. I looked around. All the fans in the bleachers were on their feet, yelling on my behalf. The ref had tried to blow his whistle, but it didn't do any good. He was fighting a losing battle. He retreated to the office on the side of the gym.

Amira had made her way over to the bleachers with Miss McKay. She'd have figured out what was going on by now. I didn't want her knowing that as great as Canada was, this was happening. I was being denied my chance to play because I was Muslim.

Josh ran over to our circle. "Mr. Letner?"

Mr. Letner turned to him.

"The team took a vote." Josh looked at me. "We aren't playing unless Sadia plays, too. We'll forfeit the game if we have to."

I didn't want to start crying, but hearing my friends chanting for me and knowing what my team was willing to sacrifice made tears well up in my eyes and tumble down my cheeks. I wiped them away, but they kept coming. Mom was crying, too, holding her hand over her mouth. I thought she was going to hug Josh.

I looked at my team. They were still shouting, "Let her play!" at the top of their voices. Jillian had pulled out her phone and was filming the whole thing, panning the bleachers and my teammates.

The ref came out of the office and went to talk to the other team. The players were looking as confused as their coach. They had a short conversation and then the ref came to the middle of the floor. He held up his hands and waited for the chanting to die down. Mr. Letner motioned for the team to sit quietly and listen. My parents and I moved against the wall. Mom and Dad each took one of my hands and held it in theirs. Mariam shot the ref a fiery look and moved close to me, as if her waifish body could protect me from his words. "I have contacted the basketball tournament officials. Even though the player's uniform is not regulation —" There was lots of booing when he said this. He had to wait until things quieted down again. "The other team has agreed to let her play." It was impossible to hear his next words because the cheering was so loud. Feet stomping, clapping, and shouting filled the gymnasium. Mom squeezed my hand and held me against her. I looked at my team through watery eyes. They could have just let me leave, but they'd been willing to stand up for me.

"The game will begin in five minutes," the ref said and nodded at the timekeeper to reset the countdown clock. Mr. Letner, Josh, Mariam, and I walked to the bench. I got hugs and high-fives from everyone on the team.

"Thanks, you guys," I said tearfully.

"We weren't going to let that happen," Jillian piped up.

"Stupid rules." Allan balled up his fists like he wanted to punch something.

Josh moved close to me. His fingers grazed mine. Was it an accident? I closed my eyes and took a deep breath. *Focus,* I told myself. I pulled my hand away and crossed my arms. I needed to concentrate on what Mr. Letner was saying, not on how close Josh was standing next to me.

"Okay," Mr. Letner said with a deep breath. We all looked at him, tense with pent-up nerves. "Kids, there's nothing I can tell you about playing as a team that you don't already know." He looked each one of us in the eyes. "Show the same kind of spirit that you just showed for Sadia when you are on the court and no one will be able to beat you." His voice turned to a low growl. "Now, get out there and win this game!"

We all cheered and put our hands in to count "Three, two, one, Thunder!"

"Hey, Mr. Letner," Josh said as he ran on the court, "I thought basketball was all about fun."

Mr. Letner shook his head. "Not anymore. Now we have something to prove in this tournament." He looked at me. "You ready?"

I met Mr. Letner's eyes. My team had stood behind me; it was time for me to show them what happens when you give a girl a basketball.

CHAPTER 21

The game had been a lot of back-and-forth play. We'd been leading for most of it, but only by a couple of points. The other team had some really strong players. No one was as tall as Jillian, but some of the boys were quick and could dribble through our defence. The other coach called a time out with a minute and thirty seconds left. I'd been subbed out, but Mr. Letner had already given me the nod that I was going in for the last shift. We had possession of the ball, so as small forward, it was going to be my job to get the ball to Jillian to see if she could use her pivot moves to score.

"Josh, you and Jillian are going to move up. Sadia, fake that you are going to pass to Josh, but look for Jillian. If she is open, pass to her. Jill, drive up and shoot. Thomas, you get ready for the rebound. We've missed a few, and I don't want to give them the chance to score." Mr. Letner stretched out his hand. We piled ours on top of it. "Three, two, one, Thunder!" we shouted in unison. The ref blew his whistle and we pounded across the court into our positions.

I slapped the ball to start the play. Josh had run

downcourt. Jillian was on the other side, flanked by two players. No matter which way she pivoted, she couldn't get free of them. Josh was open; I dribbled down to half court, taking my time. A minute and fifteen seconds was left on the clock. If we scored and the other team got the ball, they'd have a chance to get a basket and then who knew what would happen? I could wait up here and drain the clock, but eventually someone would charge me and I might lose it. *Focus,* I said to myself and took a breath. Finally, Jillian managed to get herself free. I faked a throw to Josh and sent the pass to Jillian. She dribbled once, twice, and then took a jump shot. The ball sailed into the basket. Thomas was underneath. He got the rebound and hugged it against him, then bounce-passed to Josh. Josh looked for an opening, pivoting in all directions, but couldn't get free of the players covering him. "Josh!" I called. He ducked under one guy's arm, spotted me, and tossed the ball my way. I caught it, spun around, held out my left hand to protect it, and moved up to the net. I spun and took a shot. It went in! The kids in the stands cheered. Less than thirty seconds on the clock.

The other team had possession. They started downcourt. I blocked the point guard at centre court, determined not to let him pass me. My basketball shoes squeaked with each step I took. I jammed them into the floor, holding my ground. Twenty seconds. He tried to pass to his centre; Josh intercepted and ran upcourt and scored! The other team stood, lifeless, and checked the scoreboard. We were up by eight points and there was only fifteen seconds left on the clock.

Everyone went crazy in the stands when the buzzer sounded. "One down, two to go!" Mr. Letner said as he high-fived us coming off the court. "Great effort, everyone. You played like a team." Then he looked directly at me when he said, "You showed a lot of mental grit out there. I'm proud of you." He scanned the team, and added, "All of you! Now rest up. Our next game is against the Lazers and they are tough." That news was met with excitement.

We went to centre court to shake hands with the other team and then stood in a line to hear which players were selected as MVPs by the coaches. Mr. Letner called the centre from the other team forward to receive his certificate. The other team's coach took the microphone and said, "I kinda wish we hadn't said she could play." Everyone laughed. Jillian gave me a backslap and Thomas held his fist up for a bump. "Come on over, Number Seven."

Mom stood up and snapped a photo on her phone. Dad raised his hands in triumph. "From almost not being allowed to play, to winning MVP. Pretty impressive!" Mr. Letner whispered in my ear.

But I knew it wouldn't have been possible without my team. I was lucky to have them standing beside me.

Mr. Letner ordered pizzas from the canteen and set us up in a quiet corridor to rest before our next game. A few kids lay down on their gym bags to listen to music or watch shows on their phones. Mariam went to find Amira, while Jillian, Josh, Thomas, and I sat in a circle talking. "I used to play hockey against some of the kids from the Lazers," Josh said. "They're tough."

"I heard they're dirty, too," Thomas added. Small and quick, Thomas was serious and focused when he was on the court.

"They were watching the last few minutes of the game," Jillian said. "They booed when we scored."

From down the hallway, we heard a nasty laugh. "Resting up?" a boy called. He was tall and broad, with blond hair buzzed to his scalp. He wore a Lazers warm-up jacket.

"Ugh," Josh groaned, looking to see who'd spoken. "Derek," he muttered under his breath the same way he would have if he'd found a squashed bug in his pizza.

Allan piped up. "No! But you should be. By the way, nice track suits. Does it say Lazers, or Losers?" Allan asked squinting at Derek's jacket.

Derek gave him the finger and walked back into the gym. Josh gave us a look like What did I tell you?

"Guys like him are all talk," Jillian said louder than she needed to, hoping he'd hear. Jillian might not have been intimidated by them, but I was. And she could tell when she looked at my face. She waved a dismissive hand at Derek. "Don't worry about him." I saw Mariam walking from the gym with Amira and waved. Everyone shuffled over to make room for them in the circle. Amira looked at me with bright eyes, her face more animated than usual.

"Congratulations!" she said.

I grinned back at her, relieved that after coming all this way, she'd been able to see me play *and* win.

"Was that your first basketball game?" Allan asked. I repeated the question in Arabic and Amira nodded. "What do you think?" he asked her.

"Tell him it was exciting and fun. He's a good player." Allan grinned when I relayed what she'd said. "But you're better," she said quietly to me. I didn't translate that part.

"Are you staying to watch the next game?" I asked. She shook her head no.

"Miss McKay is taking me home now. I promised my brothers I'd take them tobogganing."

I opened my eyes wide. "Good luck with that!" I said, adding a prayer in Arabic for her. I couldn't imagine trying to corral those boys on a snow hill. "Maybe if we make it into the finals tomorrow, you can come and watch. I'm really glad you could come, Amira." She grinned at me. The haunted look that had been in her eyes when she'd first arrived was fading. Bit by bit, she was settling in to her new life. She waved goodbye and went to meet Miss McKay at the front doors. She didn't shuffle meekly like she had the first day I'd shown her around the school.

"Remember how quiet she was when she first moved here? Like a scared rabbit," Mariam said, echoing my thoughts. "She seems different now."

I nodded, glad she'd noticed the change. "I think I figured out what to do for my passion project," I said. Without realizing it, we'd slipped into speaking in Arabic, something that hadn't happened in a while. She looked at me expectantly. "I want to help Amira find her friends, the ones she left behind in Syria."

Mariam looked taken aback. I guess it was an ambitious project. Not just thousands, but hundreds of thousands of people had fled Syria since the war started. Locating a couple of them would be difficult, maybe even impossible. But Mr. Letner had told us a passion project wasn't about finishing something and presenting it in a neat and tidy bow, it was about doing something that mattered.

"How are you going to do that?"

"I'm not sure," I admitted.

"I'll help you," Mariam said. "I know it's not my project, but I'd still like to do something. I wasn't as nice to her when she arrived as I should have been." Hearing Mariam say those words was like the mask she'd been wearing for the last month had fallen away. Her voice dropped and she got pensive. "I think she reminded me of who I was when I arrived. All that not knowing, I hated it." Mariam winced. "I didn't want to go back to that; the awkwardness. It brought up lots of memories I wanted to forget."

"We were never like her; we weren't refugees." I knew more about what Amira had been through than Mariam did, but now wasn't the time to tell her.

Mr. Letner's If You Give a Kid a Camera project had been about taking photos that showed our perspective of the world, what mattered to us. I wondered what photos Amira would pick. Part of me wanted her to show people what life was really like for refugees moving to Canada. In Syria, her dad, an engineer, had been able to support his family, but now they had to rely on donations and live crammed together in a two-bedroom apartment.

But another part of me wanted Amira to show the flip side. Amidst all the turmoil, her family was adapting to their new life and finding a way to make Canada their home. There was relief that they'd made it. Slowly, she was figuring out how to move past what she'd lived through. It had changed her, but it hadn't broken her.

The pizza Mr. Letner had ordered for the team wasn't halal, but I'd planned ahead and brought my own lunch. As the rest of the team swarmed the food, Mariam's parents called her away. "Here we go," she said with a dramatic sigh. "I wonder what I've done wrong now." I watched as they both hovered over her, leaning in close. Mom claimed their strict rules were more about protecting their daughter than trying to ruin her life, but Mariam would argue differently. She shot me a look of wide-eyed irritation as she walked back.

"In their continued effort to isolate me, my parents are taking me for lunch." Mariam blinked at me, her frustration evident. "Please join us," she said through gritted teeth.

My parents knew I wouldn't want to leave and had gone for lunch without me. I scrunched up my nose. "I think I should stay with the team."

"I wish I could." Mariam cast a woeful look at everyone laughing and digging in to the pizza. Two grease-stained boxes already sat empty. "On the upside" — her tone changed — "they're going home after lunch and asked your parents to drive me home. And," she paused dramatically, "they said I could sleep over at your house tomorrow if it's all right with your parents." She raised her lips with a hint of a smile.

Even though she hadn't mentioned Jillian's party since this morning, the topic was simmering beneath the surface. She wasn't the type of person to let something drop.

"Please, Sadia?" She clutched my arm. "It's a good plan. I promise I won't ask you to cover for me again."

I doubted that, but she'd backed me into a corner. Saying no could put us back to where we'd been a few weeks ago. And the truth was, I *did* want to go and not just because of Josh. I wanted to hang out with my team. The older kids there were probably going to be drinking, but it wasn't going to be forced on me.

What Mom and Dad didn't know wouldn't hurt them. Wasn't that Aazim's way of thinking, too?

"Fine," I groaned. "I'll ask." I barely got the words out before she gave an excited squeal.

As Mariam walked to meet her mom and dad at the front hall, I thought about the murky days we'd had. The chasm between us widened and closed. Maybe that was a normal part of friendship now. It wasn't a concrete wall, strong and secure, like it had been when we were younger. It was more flexible, with gaps and spots to jump over. I couldn't expect Mariam to stay the same forever. It was normal that she change. I guess I was changing, too; I just couldn't see it.

"Where's Mariam going?" Josh asked as I sat down. I pulled some food out of my backpack.

"Her parents are taking her for lunch."

Josh twisted around to watch them go.

"Do you ever go watch your brother play out of town?" I asked. His comment about his parents choosing to watch his brother's game and miss the basketball tournament, coupled with the photo he'd shown in class, made me curious about his family.

"Only if he has a game in the city. When he played Triple A, I used to go all the time."

I didn't know the levels of hockey, but I assumed Triple A was good if he was going to be drafted. "Did you play?"

A dark look crossed his face.

"Till he quit," Allan piped up. I hadn't realized he'd been listening to our conversation. "Who wins the city championship and then quits hockey?" He shook his head in disbelief.

"Did you like hockey?"

"Yeah, loved it."

I frowned, not understanding. "So why did you stop playing?"

"It stopped being fun."

Allan raised an eyebrow and snorted like he didn't agree, but Josh gave him a look like he should keep quiet. The perennial grin that Josh wore had disappeared. He cleared his throat and lowered his voice. "You saw the photo of my dad. He's really intense and I was never going to go as far as Max." He shrugged as if that explained things. He tossed his half-eaten pizza crust into the box and took a long swig of water. A droplet hung on his lip and he wiped it away with the back of his hand.

When he looked back at me again, the grin had returned. "Basketball's more fun, anyway," he said, but I wondered if he just told himself that or if he really believed it.

CHAPTER 22

We walked into the gym fifteen minutes before game time. The game before us was almost finished, and the score was so lopsided, I felt bad for the losing team. Nobody wanted to be beat by thirty points. The Lazers were on the other side of the gym in their matching warm-up suits doing jumping jacks in unison. Jillian rolled her eyes at them, which made me laugh. I was looking forward to a tough game, and one that didn't involve drama over my outfit like the first game had.

We had the same ref as our other game. He ran over to speak to Mr. Letner, his whistle bouncing against his chest. Mr. Letner bowed to listen to him and then nodded. I watched as the ref ran along the sidelines to speak to the Lazers coach. Mr. Letner came back to our bench. "The ref is asking the Lazers coach about your uniform," he said quietly to me. The other coach was a tall, burly man with a moustache. As the ref explained the issue with my uniform, the coach smirked and crossed his arms over his chest.

We both watched in disbelief as the coach shook his head.

He wasn't going to let me play. I turned to Mr. Letner. "Now what?"

Mr. Letner stiffened. "Let's hear what the ref says." But I heard the frustration in his voice and saw the way he narrowed his eyes, glaring at the other team's bench.

The ref came back to Mr. Letner and cleared his throat. His eyes flickered to my face regretfully. "Sorry. Uh, he said no, he doesn't agree that she can play in her current uniform. She'll have to change into regulation clothing or be removed from the roster for this game."

Mr. Letner threw his hands in the air and sputtered in disbelief. "*This* is the kind of tournament you want to run?"

"I'm sorry." The ref sighed and frowned. "If it were up to me, she'd play. We're already bending the rules. I can't overrule him."

Across the gym, the Lazers coach had a smug look on his face. He knew it would rattle our team when they found out I couldn't play. Luckily, everyone else was still preoccupied with the game on the court to notice our conversation. I set my chin with determination. "It's okay, Mr. Letner," I said. "I played the first game. I'll sit this one out."

Mr. Letner shook his head. "They're playing dirty," he said. "They know we're better than them and they're looking for an advantage." He gave me a long look. "The team will fight for you, if you want them, too. They'd rather not play than play without you."

"I know. But this time, I think they should just play and not worry about me. I don't want to be a distraction."

"Other coaches will be more reasonable." Mr. Letner seethed. "You'll get to play the third game today."

"And then the playoffs tomorrow," I added.

He took a deep breath. "You're sure this is what you want to do? Because I can ask the team —"

"I'm sure," I said and nodded. I didn't want to sacrifice our chance at playoffs because the Lazers won by default.

Mr. Letner clapped a hand on my shoulder and called the team over. "Okay, team, huddle up!" He leaned down, eye level with all of us. "I've got some bad news —"

"That we have to play a bunch of assholes?" Allan interrupted.

Mr. Letner looked at Allan, but didn't argue. "Sadia isn't playing this game. The Lazers coach said he wouldn't allow it."

His words were met with an uproar. "What?" "No!" "That's not fair!"

"Listen," Mr. Letner looked everyone in the eye. "This is part of the Lazers plan. They want to throw us off-kilter. We can't let them get to us."

I took a deep breath and swallowed back the lump of disappointment that had formed in my throat. I didn't want my team, or the Lazers, to see how upset I was. In the stands, mom and dad were talking excitedly with other parents. What would they do when they saw me sitting on the sidelines? "They're being racist," Jillian said. She looked like she was ready to explode.

"That may be, but they want to win the game, whatever it takes —"

"We aren't going to let them," Josh promised.

"That's right." Mr. Letner gave him a grim smile. "We aren't. Sadia would prefer that you play without her than give them a win by default." I nodded to show my agreement, but his words were met with silence.

"Seriously, you guys. I want you to play." It took everything I had to keep my voice strong and even.

The team looked at each other doubtfully. "You're sure?" Josh asked.

I gave a confident nod. "I'll be sitting right here, cheering you on."

"We'll win it for you, Sadia," Mohammed said and the whole team nodded. Mariam threw the Lazers a dirty look.

The time clock said five minutes till game time. Mr. Letner passed everyone balls, including me, to warm-up. "The coach is a jerk. He probably saw how good you were. He thinks we can't win without you," Josh said to me.

"You can," I said.

Our basketballs pounded the hardwood floors. I blinked back tears and refused to look in the other team's direction. It wasn't fair, what they were doing, but I was glad my team wasn't going to sacrifice the game for me. Not against a team of cheaters like the Lazers.

When the buzzer rang and warm-up was over, I ran past my parents, but didn't look at them. If they saw my face they'd know something was wrong. I put my ball away and went to sit on the bench between Mariam and Mr. Letner. The rest of the team huddled around, waiting to find out the game plan. Since I wasn't playing, Mr. Letner moved Thomas to small forward. Jillian and Josh would play centre on two lines. "Don't let them intimidate you. We're a stronger team, and we have something more important. Heart."

As soon as the ref blew the whistle, I dug my fingernails into my palms. When the second line went out and I stayed on the bench, I saw my parents turn and look at each other. Their confusion turned to anger when I caught their eyes and shook my head. I thought Dad was going to leap off the bleachers. Thankfully, Mom tugged his sleeve and whispered something in his ear. She knew arguing wouldn't do any good. Watching the team play without being on the court was stressful. The Lazers were aggressive and pushed and shoved their way through our defence. Mariam had already pulled two ice packs out of the first-aid cooler Mr. Letner had brought.

We were down by ten until Josh came back with a three-pointer and then another. Shane scored on two foul shots and the game was tied up. There was still five minutes left to play. My feet jittered on the bench. I didn't know how Mr. Letner stayed calm watching us. He remained almost silent, only shouting, "Good play!" or "Nice D!" to the team. Meanwhile, the Lazers coach was beet-red in his face and looked like his eyeballs wanted to pop out of his head. He didn't shut up. Only his comments weren't always supportive. "Open your eyes!" "We won't win if you play like that!" and my favourite, "Crush them!" rang out across the court. He slapped his clipboard against his thighs a couple of times, too. Once I thought he was going to throw it at his players when Mohammed danced around them and set Jillian up with a perfect shot.

"Stay focused," Mr. Letner said when he called a time out with two minutes left. The Lazers were up by two points. It was hard to pay attention to what he was saying as the other coach ranted at his players. Mr. Letner outlined the play. "Thomas is going to drive to the net. Everyone else support him, call for the ball. Communicate! You guys got this," he said.

The team took their positions, jogging on the spot to keep warmed up. The ref blew the whistle and the Lazers ran to the court. Their centre sneered at Allan. "Kinda chubby to be playing ball, aren't you?" Allan narrowed his eyes at him and looked like he was going to make a smart retort, but he bit his tongue. "That your girlfriend over there?" The Lazers centre nodded to me. "She so ugly they have to cover her up?"

I almost choked hearing his nasty words. The worst part was, he *meant* for me to hear them. Even though he'd been speaking to Allan, Josh balled his hands up into fists. His face went a darker shade of red.

"Let's go, Thunder!" I cheered, trying to distract Allan and Josh. Maybe hearing my voice would remind them why they were out there. Jillian won the toss and passed the ball to Thomas. He drove to the net, just like Mr. Letner had told him to do. The mouthy kid blocked the shot and got the ball. He ran down the court and scored. Mr. Letner scratched his head, his mouth twitching with disappointment. Our ball. Rory put it in play and passed to Allan, but the same kid stood in front of him. I saw his lips move; he said something, but I couldn't make out what it was. Allan's eyes got big and his lips curled. He shoved the kid out of his way and looked to make a pass, but the ref called foul. Allan's head went back as he groaned. "No way! You didn't hear what he said to me!"

"Allan!" Mr. Letner shouted. Allan turned his way and Mr. Letner shook his head, a silent reminder to respect the ref. Allan screwed up his face and shouldered past the Lazers players to get into position for the foul shot. The Lazers players on the bench got to their feet and chanted, "Lou! Lou! Lou!"

"Guess his name is Lou," I muttered under my breath. He took the shot and it went in. The Lazers were up by five points. Mariam was almost hoarse from yelling encouragement to the team, but even her energy was failing. Only twenty seconds left. One more chance for our team, but the ball was stolen out of Thomas's hands. By the time the buzzer went, our team was deflated. Everyone trudged to the bench.

"Do we have to shake hands with them?" Allan asked.

"Come on, kids. You're better than them, in every way. We'll get 'em next time." Mr. Letner led the way and we lined up to congratulate them. Not one Lazer said "Good game." They looked straight ahead as if they were better than us.

"Assholes," Jillian muttered under her breath.

"Told you to rest up," Derek called to Josh.

Josh gritted his teeth. At first, I thought he was going to ignore the comment, but then he turned around, seething. "Guess you guys were too scared of Sadia to let her play, huh? Maybe next time, you'll let our *whole* team play."

Josh's comment was met by a series of jibes about me being his girlfriend. I swallowed back my own comments and tried to pull Josh away. "This is what they want us to do," I said quietly.

But then Mariam piped up. "It's true. You hid behind some discriminatory rule to keep her out of the game. You're all a bunch of cowards!"

The Lazers scoffed at Mariam, looking her up and down, taking in her hijab with a sneer. It wasn't overtly racist, but it riled the rest of us.

"You want to take this outside?" Allan shouted at them.

Mr. Letner grabbed Allan's shoulder and propelled him to the exit. "Let's get some air, kids. That game was a little intense."

"I hope the next game goes better," Mohammed muttered to me as we left the gym.

"Me, too," I agreed. *And that I'm on the court playing and not on the sidelines watching,* I added to myself.

CHAPTER 23

Our third game was against the Lightning, which sounded funny: Thunder versus Lightning. The Lightning coach agreed to let me play before the ref even asked. I guess word had spread. We won easily, but after the loss to the Lazers, we came in second in the pool of six teams, which meant we had to play the third-place team in the morning to get to the finals.

After the game, Mr. Letner sent Mariam to the bulletin board to wait for tomorrow's games to be posted on the playoff tree. The team relaxed on the benches, too tired to move. Josh was beside me, only a breath of air separating our bodies. Mine, even fully covered, felt charged with him so close. *What am I doing?* I asked myself. I shifted away from him. I had to say something — I couldn't let things keep going like this.

"So you're going to Jillian's party —" he started but was interrupted as everyone's attention turned to Mariam. The tail of her scarf waved behind her like a banner as she marched down the hallway. I wasn't sure I wanted to hear the rest of what he had to say, anyway.

"We play at eight a.m. against the Celtics," she said.

"Eight a.m.?" a few people groaned. "That's so early on a Sunday!" Jeein said.

"Ten p.m. curfew tonight!" Mr. Letner said.

Everyone collected their bags and went to find their rides home. "Hey, guys, wait up." Jillian bounded across the floor, catching up with Mariam and me in a few steps. Even worn out, she moved faster than most people at full energy. My parents were waiting with Jillian's mom at the entrance. They must have been tired, too. Except for leaving at lunch, they'd been hanging around the sportsplex for as long as I had been. "What a game, girls!" Jillian's mother looked just like her daughter, only with some grey hair mixed with the blond. "Everyone played great."

"And you're going to miss watching us play tomorrow to go skiing!" Jillian lamented. Mrs. Triggs gave her a pained look.

"Maybe I should call Dad and change things around."

"No!" Jillian said quickly. "You should go skiing. I'm just bugging you."

Her mom still looked doubtful, but Jillian reassured her. "Seriously, Mom! It's okay! They'll be other tournaments."

Mrs. Triggs turned to my parents. "Poor Jill. She's our third. We used to be such good parents," she said with a self-deprecating laugh.

"Yeah, till Julia wore you down." Their banter made me think they'd joked about this before. Jillian gave me a knowing look. "I look like an angel compared to her."

Considering Julia was the sister throwing the party tomorrow night, I didn't doubt it.

"At least we're at a stage now where I can trust all three of you," Mrs. Triggs said.

Jillian didn't flinch at the irony of her mom's comment. I shot a worried look at Mariam, who stared at Jillian with wide-eyed fascination. Mrs. Triggs smiled at all of us. Her gaze landed on Mariam. "Were you playing, too?" she asked.

Mariam shook her head. "No. I'm the team manager."

"She's also the one who designed and sewed Sadia's outfit."

Jillian's mom looked impressed. "You're so talented!" she gushed. Mariam smiled and shrugged her shoulders like it was nothing.

"A bunch of kids in Mr. Letner's homeroom are doing passion projects. That was Mariam's." Jillian turned to me. "What's yours?"

"I'm still trying to figure it out."

"Winning the tournament?" Jillian joked. She hiked her gym bag up on her shoulder. "Kay, see you guys tomorrow!" We waved goodbye. The crowd at the entrance had started to thin out.

"A passion project? What is that?" Dad asked as we walked to the car.

"It's not for marks," I quickly assured him. "We are supposed to come up with something we care about so much we don't mind working on it on our own time."

Dad made a noise in his throat and did a "hmm, interesting" face, which is also the same as his frowning face. His moustache dipped down and his forehead wrinkled. "And what is your idea?" he asked me. We walked across the parking lot to our car, our breath visible in the cold night air.

"I know my idea, I just don't know how to make it happen."

"Tell me, maybe I can help."

I looked at him doubtfully. "Okay," I started. And as I explained to him how Amira had left her friends behind and didn't know where they'd gone, or even if they were still alive, his gaze got more intense. "It's a good idea. A great idea!" Dad said as he got into the car. Mariam nodded in agreement.

"I know, but how can I make it happen?"

Dad turned on the car and let the engine warm up. "Hmmm, well, let's think about it and see what we can come up with." I thought about the science projects I'd handed in as a kid and how Dad used to enjoy working on them as much as I did. Mom had had a wistful look on her face as I explained my project. We were fortunate that so much of our family had already left Syria before the war started. But Mom had also left a job she loved and co-workers and friends. I knew she'd lost touch with them and worried about their whereabouts. Figuring out how to help all people who'd lost loved ones, not just refugees, would be useful.

Dad turned the heat on full blast as we pulled out of the parking lot.

"You missed prayers today," Mom said.

"I know.... What about you?" I asked.

"Dad and I found a spot. A multi-purpose room." Dad packed a prayer mat in his car, just for occasions like that. Mom swivelled in her seat so she was facing me. "I was so proud of you today, Sadia. You, too, Mariam." She swallowed, emotion making it hard to talk. "So proud."

"It was the team. They fought for me."

"You'd given them something to fight for. That's what I meant. Wait until Aazim hears."

Aazim. I'd been so preoccupied with the tournament, I'd almost forgotten that tonight was his first performance. I hated the thought of him getting up onstage without his family there to support him. He was worried Mom and Dad wouldn't understand how much acting meant to him, but I had faith in them. Moving to Canada had been a risk, the same way it was a risk for Aazim to get up onstage. I couldn't sit at home tonight, knowing my brother was the lead in a play without anyone there to watch him. The university was a half-hour away, at least. His play started at seven o'clock. If Dad drove straight there, we'd catch it. "Dad," I started, "Aazim has a surprise for you and Mom. He's been working really hard on it."

Mom looked at me, confused. "What?"

"It's a surprise. But we have to go to the university."

"Does it have to be now? I'd like to get home," Dad said. "I'm hungry."

"It has to be now."

In the rear-view mirror, I saw Dad wrinkle his forehead. "How long will it take?"

"An hour?" I guessed, even though the play would probably be longer.

"Sadia, what is it?" Mom's tone turned sharp. After a long day at the tournament, she wasn't in the mood for secrets.

"Please, just trust me. Aazim asked that I not tell you until we get there." The lie slid quickly off my tongue.

The two of them exchanged a look, but relented. My phone buzzed with a text. It was from Mariam. *What's going on?*

Aazim is in a play at university. He's worried Mom and Dad will be mad.

But you're taking them?

Yes, I thumbed back to her. Mariam widened her eyes, giving me a look that suggested I was crazy. A hint of doubt crept into my head. What if they were upset at him for keeping the secret? Or told him he couldn't act anymore?

I pushed the doubts aside. My parents weren't like that. Once they saw Aazim onstage and realized that he was following his passion and taking a chance, they would be proud of him.

Dad parked in his assigned spot beside his faculty. The old buildings were covered with ivy in the summer, but now bare vines scrolled around their stone facades. "Now where?" he asked when we got out of the toasty warm car and stepped into the chilly winter night.

While we were driving, I'd pulled up some information about the play on my phone. "*Some Dark Day.* Written by Kareem Siddiqi. Starring Aazim Ahmadi." There was a list of other actors' names after his, but Aazim's was the only one I cared about. "7:00 p.m., doors open at 6:30 p.m. Parker Theatre, Isbister Building."

"The Isbister Building," I told him.

He thought for a moment. "That's this way," he said. "In the arts complex." For the tenth time, he threw me a confused look. "What is going on?" he mumbled under his breath.

"Trust me. You'll be happy we came," I replied. We trudged along a snowy path. In the car, they'd tried guessing everything from a surprise party for their anniversary (which was in July!) to visiting a relative.

"Is this something for school? For this passion project?" Dad asked.

"Kind of. You'll see when we get there." *Not my passion project, Aazim's!*

"Your parents are good sports," Mariam whispered to me as we walked. "There's no way my parents would go along with this."

A crowd had formed on the steps of a building that looked more like a castle than a university building. It even had a rounded turret on one side. Posters advertising the play were stapled to the board outside. I waited for Mom or Dad to notice Aazim's name, but neither of them did. We might be in our seats before they realized why we were there. By then, it would be too late for them to leave. I didn't think they would, but that seed of doubt still lay in my head.

Mom and Dad looked at me. "Why are we here? Where is your brother?" Mom asked. Mariam glanced around, wide-eyed and curious. A faint smile curled her lips when she saw the poster.

"Come on," I said and headed for the stairs into the building. "You'll understand once we are inside."

A line had formed at the box office and I joined it. Mom and Dad were really curious now, looking around, trying to figure out why their daughter had dragged them here. "Look," I said and pointed to a poster for the play. They peered at it. Mom read Aazim's name first; her jaw opened in surprise. "Aazim?" she whispered. Dad saw it, too, and turned to me, startled.

"What's going on?"

"Aazim's the lead!" I said. "He's been rehearsing for weeks. Tonight is the first show!"

They both stared at me in shock. Mom's eyebrows knit together. "How is this possible? He has his studies."

"*And* he's been doing this play."

Dad pressed his lips together and glared at me. "Aazim should not be wasting his time on this."

"But —"

"No. This is not appropriate."

"Why not?"

"He's going to be a doctor." Mom kept her voice low. "His school work should be his focus."

"He can do this, too," I pointed out as the line moved closer to the box office. "Please, we're here. Can't we stay and watch him?" I pleaded. They both looked angry enough to storm away. I wondered if having Mariam with us helped. They had to keep up appearances.

"Why did he keep this a secret?" Mom asked me.

"He was worried about what you'd say."

"Because he knew it was a waste of time." Dad huffed and dug his hands into his pockets. "I hope his grades haven't suffered because of this."

I cringed at Dad's words and what he would do when he found out Aazim had dropped some courses. "What if he's really good? You'll regret saying these things." It was almost our turn to buy tickets. A girl in hijab with large, dark, kohl-rimmed eyes and an open face sat at the desk. She asked Dad in lightly accented English how many tickets he'd like. "Four," was his gruff response. He put his money on the table and she carefully slid the change back to him, making sure to lay the money on the counter rather than put it in his hands. I wondered if this girl was part of the reason Aazim had auditioned for the play. I caught Mariam's eye and knew she was thinking the same thing.

We went through the doors and into the theatre. It was a small space with about eighty seats on three sides. Dad led the way and found us four seats together in the centre of the fourth row from the stage. I worried about Aazim seeing us. What if it threw him off?

"Call your parents," Mom whispered to Mariam. "They might be worried that you're not home yet."

"I already texted them," Mariam said. "They said no problem as long as I am home by ten o'clock."

We sat quietly, waiting for the show to begin. The rest of the seats filled up, and hushed chatter filled the theatre. The stage was sparse, made to look like a classroom, with student desks and a blackboard. Music started, a haunting violin song, and the lights dimmed. I held my hands tightly in my lap, excited to see my brother.

When he got onstage, I wanted to stand up and cheer. He was wearing jeans, a button-down shirt, and a cardigan. His hair was combed so it lay shiny and flat against his head. His opening lines were all Aazim; his voice and his mannerisms. At first I couldn't separate the two, but as the play went on, I forgot it was my brother up there. He embodied the character he played, losing himself in the moments onstage. At one point, after a moving monologue, he looked into the audience. I thought he'd seen us, but the lights at centre stage were blindingly bright. We were probably still faceless members of the audience. I glanced at Mom; her face was pulled tight with emotion.

The play was about a school shooting. Aazim played a teacher trying to protect his students and talk the shooter, a racist white man who blamed immigration for his personal problems, into surrendering. Aazim and the other actor spent most of the time onstage in a heated debate.

Eventually, Aazim's character was able to convince the guy to give up the gun just as the police crashed in. Seeing a Muslim man with a gun, they assumed Aazim's character was the gunman and shot him. I gasped. Aazim went down with a crash. A soundtrack of children screaming played as the lights went dark.

I was so caught up in the play that tears sprang to my eyes. *No!* I wanted to shout. *You can't end it like that!* I sat stunned in my seat. No one in the audience moved; we sat reeling from the final, shocking scene.

When the house lights flooded on, Aazim and the cast held hands and bowed to our applause. A lump formed in my throat and my eyes welled with teary pride as I watched Aazim take a second bow on his own. The crowd got to their feet for an ovation that left my hands sore. He was the star of the show. His role demanded so much emotion and empathy; it was heartbreaking.

I turned to Mom and Dad. I didn't have to ask them what they thought; they were both wiping their eyes. Dad sniffled and cleared his throat.

"He was so good!" Mariam said. "Aazim was amazing!"

I didn't trust myself to speak, so I nodded.

As the audience rose and left their seats, we waited, collecting ourselves.

The play had left me shaken, and not just because of Aazim's perfomance. I thought about Mom while she'd been waiting for the bus a few weeks ago; what the man had yelled at her, and the woman's racist remarks. And I thought about the way the woman had stared at me as I got on the bus. What had she been thinking about me? When I though about it, the ending of the play was horrifying, but not unrealistic. Maybe that was part of the reason Aazim was so determined to be part of it.

The cast came out to greet their families. I spotted Aazim in the middle of a crowd of well-wishers congratulating him on his performance. The girl from the box office hovered near him.

A man wearing a blazer and thick-framed glasses came to pump Aazim's hand. He slapped his other arm and shook his head in admiration. "It was more than I hoped for!" I heard him proclaim.

"Who is that?" Mariam whispered beside me.

I shrugged. "The director? The writer?"

"No, not him, the girl!"

She'd slipped beside Aazim, comfortably. Warning

bells rang in my head. Seeing Aazim onstage was enough of a shock. What would my parents do if they realized he was dating someone as well? No wonder he didn't want to give me advice on Josh! I bustled in front of Dad, leading the way toward the stage. "Aazim!" I called out. He looked at me like he couldn't believe what he was seeing.

"Sadia!"

"We came!"

His face paled as he realized Mom and Dad were behind me. My eyes went to the girl beside him, but she'd already taken a step back and turned to talk to someone else.

"You were incredible!" I gushed. "That play was intense! You made me cry." I threw my arms around his neck. "I couldn't *not* come," I whispered in his ear. "I needed to see —"

He unwrapped my arms and glared at me. "I told you not to!"

"It's okay, they loved it. They loved you." We turned to look at Mom and Dad. They stood awkwardly, waiting to talk to Aazim. Mariam had stayed back at the edge of the stage. I moved toward her, but Aazim pulled me back. It was like a standoff: Mom and Dad against the two of us. I thought Dad would speak first, but it was Mom who finally said, "We should go. We'll see you at home." She turned on her heel and left, Dad at her side.

I stared at them and turned back to Aazim. His face fell. "I knew it," he muttered. "You shouldn't have brought them."

"But they loved it. I saw their faces!"

He gave me a steely glare. "Go." The sharpness of

his words cut me. With pleading eyes, I begged him to understand why I'd wanted them to see his play. "Please, go, Sadia." He turned away and ducked into the backstage. The girl shot a quick glance my way and retreated after him, the darkness swallowing them both up.

CHAPTER 24

The car ride home was silent. Mom and Dad stared out the windshield. Snow crunched under the tires as we turned into Mariam's driveway to drop her off. The light was on over her front door. Mariam got out of the car and Dad lowered his window to shout a greeting to Mr. Hassanin, who came to the door. Once Mariam was safely inside, Dad reversed out of the driveway and the mood in the car completely changed. All the pent-up emotion came flooding out.

"How has he found the time for this?" Mom wailed.

"Does it matter? He was amazing." They were silent, which I took for reluctant agreement.

"His acting abilities are not what I'm worried about," Dad snorted. "But if this has affected his studies ..." Dad's voice trailed off warningly. "Why did he keep it a secret?"

Dad glared at me in the rear-view mirror, as if he was trying to coax me to confess what I knew. "He was worried you'd react like *this*." I took a deep breath and tried a different approach. "You let him play basketball, how is this any different?"

Dad scoffed. "That was in high school! He's in university now. His studies come first, not parading around a stage. When he has his degree and a career, he can do what he likes, but for now, school comes first."

"Acting won't help him get into medical school. When you have children, you'll understand," Mom replied. I fell back against the seat. It was useless to argue with them.

When we arrived home, Aazim's car was already in the driveway. Driving Mariam home had delayed us. I said a silent prayer that things would work out as I slammed my car door and followed my parents into the house in a brooding procession.

Aazim was sitting at the kitchen table with a glass of water. "Sadia, go to your room," Mom commanded. I threw a look at Aazim. His head was bowed and he didn't look up. He'd have to admit he'd dropped class to rehearse and they'd be furious. My heart clenched for him. I hadn't meant to get him in trouble.

I left my door open, but all I could hear was their regular voices. My greatest fear was that they might forbid Aazim from acting in the next performances. I wouldn't be able to live with the guilt if they did that. I swore I wouldn't play basketball if they punished him that way.

But Aazim was an adult, I reasoned. What kind of parents would they be if they told him he had to drop out of the play? He wasn't hurting anyone. He'd gone behind their backs, but that crime didn't deserve such a severe a punishment, did it? I strained to hear their conversation. When I heard footsteps climbing the stairs,

I scurried to my bed in case it was Mom or Dad. But it was Aazim who walked in front of my door. I jumped up to follow him. I needed to see his face to know everything was all right.

"Aazim?"

He paused in his doorway, but didn't turn around.

"What happened?"

"Don't concern yourself," he said coldly. "You've done enough." He walked into his room and slammed his door.

I barely slept, and when my alarm rang at six-thirty in the morning, I felt like I'd been tossing and turning all night. I delayed seeing my parents for as long as possible, heading downstairs just before we needed to leave. Mom and Dad were sitting at the kitchen table, drinking tea. They both looked up when I came downstairs.

"We'll leave in ten minutes," Dad said tersely.

"Eat something," Mom said. "Did you pray?"

I had, on a prayer mat on the floor of my room. I had put a lot of heart into it, too, hoping my prayers would be answered. I wanted to do well in the tournament today, but even more, I wanted to know that Aazim would be allowed to continue with his play.

"Is Aazim —"

"Don't worry about your brother."

"I just want to know if he's coming —"

"He has to study."

"What about tonight?" I pressed. "Will he be in the play?" I knew I was pushing it. If I was smart, I'd stop asking questions, but I couldn't help myself.

Mom gave me an exasperated look. "Of course, he'll be in his play. We aren't tyrants, Sadia."

"So you aren't mad?"

She sighed. "We're disappointed. He should have talked to us about it first."

"He'll take his summer courses," Dad said. "Get caught up and apply for medical school in the fall. After this play is over, he will focus on what really matters."

Acting does *really matter to him*, I wanted to say, but didn't.

I gave a relieved sigh, not just for Aazim, but for me, too. Knowing that Aazim wasn't being punished, I could leave for the tournament with a clear conscience.

Dad grabbed the newspaper off the front steps and met Mom and I in the car. Mom had packed me lunch, a bag full of snacks to eat during the day, and my water bottle. "Are you staying the whole day?" I asked. It was an elimination playoff round. If we lost, we'd be out, but if we won, we'd play again in the finals at one o'clock.

"We were planning to. We might leave for a while when you have your break."

We had to pick Mariam up first, and as we drove, thoughts of Jillian's party crept into my mind. After the debacle with Aazim and his play, I was nervous to push things with Mom and Dad. As much as I wanted to go to the party, was lying to them worth it?

Mariam was waiting in her front window when we pulled into the driveway. It was still dark out, the sky purplish with early morning light. Mariam ran to the car. She was wearing an emerald-green head scarf today that made her light eyes sparkle. "Thanks for picking me up," she said.

She shot me a questioning look when she got in the car. I raised one shoulder in a shrug and gave her a lop-sided smile. I regretted the trouble I'd created for Aazim, but I didn't regret seeing his play. Just thinking about it, the intensity of the story and how my brother had looked on stage, gave me shivers.

Even though a lot of teams had been knocked out of playoffs during the round robin play, the sportsplex was still full of activity. Four teams were left in our age division and we were one of them. A trophy table had been moved to the front entrance. Hiking my gym bag up on my shoulder, I moved close to admire them. The three tournament trophies gleamed like golden towers. The first place trophy had a person on the top of it in a frozen jump shot. Underneath was a plaque that read "First Place Junior Varsity All-City Basketball Tournament." The plaque on a smaller one read "Finalist Junior Varsity All-City Basketball Tournament." The last one was much shorter and had a golden basket-ball on it. It read, "Junior Varsity All-City Basketball Tournament MVP." "Wow," I said, looking at them. My eyes lingered on the first place trophy. How good would it feel to hold that trophy in my hands?

Despite the early start, there were still lots of peo-ple in the gym. From the doors, I scanned the bleach-ers for kids from school. "Is Carmina coming?" I asked Mariam.

"She couldn't get a ride until later. *When* you win your first game, I'll text her and she and a bunch of other people are coming for the finals," Mariam said.

I looked at her, impressed and grateful.

"About Jillian's party," she started.

Here we go again, I thought. Had she been up all night strategizing? Before she could say anything else, I interrupted her. "Why are you obsessing about it?"

She looked at me, hurt. "I'm not."

"You are!" My nerves were frazzled, and getting into another discussion about sneaking out and lying was going to distract me.

"You don't get it," she muttered.

With an impatient sigh, I waited for her to continue. "I'm always going to be left out. If my parents had it their way, I'd finish high school without ever going to a party. At least your parents let you have a life. You're on the basketball team and have all these new friends."

I got a glimpse of things from Mariam's perspective: I was part of the team and my parents wouldn't say no to the party at Jillian's, as long as they thought it was for the team. Mariam was literally watching from the sidelines as I drifted further away from her with my basketball friends.

I knew how it had hurt to see her and Carmina getting closer. I put myself in Mariam's shoes and imagined what it would be like if she were the one getting invited to parties I knew I couldn't go to. All this time, I thought Mariam was pulling away from me, but now I saw that she was worried I'd get new experiences and she'd be left in the dust.

"Missing one party won't mean you're left out," I consoled her.

"It's not one party. It'll be *every* party. You're going to have fun and I'll be sitting at home. Alone." Her eyes filled with tears.

I heard the desperation in her voice. Was it worth lying to Mom and Dad to make her feel better? "I'll make sure you can come to the party," I said reluctantly. "I promise."

Mariam bit her lip and nodded. "Thank you," she whispered and looked like she wanted to hug me.

Mr. Letner came over and handed Mariam the game sheet. "Time to work," Mariam mumbled, blinking away the tears. She sat down to fill it out with our names and numbers and I wandered over to the rest of the team. Josh moved beside me. "I'm nervous," he whispered.

"Me, too," I whispered back. I could feel my nerves kicking in. I wanted this win, badly. If for nothing else than to prove that a girl wearing hijab belonged on the court.

Mr. Letner herded us to the bench in the gym along the wall. "Good morning, Thunder!" he announced when the team was sitting down. Today's ref wasn't the same one as yesterday, but he'd obviously been told about me because he came to speak to Mr. Letner, telling him the same rules applied today: as long as the opposing team's coach agreed, I could play.

I held my breath and tried not to look desperate while he went to the Celtic team's coach. What if she was like the Lazers coach and realized the advantage her team would have over mine if I didn't play?

But right away, she looked over at our team and grinned.

The ref jogged over. "Number Seven is in!" I let out my breath as the team cheered and high-fived me.

"Okay, team, let's get focused!" Mr. Letner began his pep talk. "We are one game away from making it to the tournament final," he began. "You play like a team, you'll win like a team!" His eyes were shining as he looked at each one of us in turn. "I've seen some amazing passing, shooting, and defense from you kids. But most of all, I've seen heart. Play your hardest out there, not just for you, but for the kids on the court with you." He finished by stretching his hand out. Josh was the first one to put his hand on top, then Allan, then me and all the other kids.

"Three, two, one, Thunder!" we yelled.

We hadn't played the Celtics in the round robin. They'd also lost to the Lazers, but had still come in third. It was clear at the first tip-off that we had a stronger team. We scored three baskets in a row in the first two minutes and dominated for the rest of the first period. But after half-time, the momentum shifted. We couldn't make a shot to save our lives! With five minutes to go, the Celtics had tied the game.

Mr. Letner called a time out. I looked up in the stands for Mom and Dad. They were literally sitting on the edge of their seats — the excitement of the game was contagious.

"It's going to come down to the wire," Mr. Letner said. "The other team doesn't want to go home either. I need fast, sharp plays. Jill, keep it tight and on the inside. Sadia, you need to keep shooting."

We nodded as the buzzer drowned out Mr. Letner. The time out was over. We just had to get ahead of the other team by one point to make the finals. In the end, Jeein won it for us with a shot from outside the key that sealed it with a swish. Our whole team came off the bench when the buzzer went off. We were going to the finals!

I saw Mom and Dad stand up and cheer as we moved through the handshake line. "You've got a good team," the other coach said to Mr. Letner. "We almost had you."

"Yeah, it was a great game. Good luck!"

"You, too."

As we packed up our bags and water bottles, the Lazers marched past us to the other bench. They were playing the fourth-place team. The winner would meet us in the championship game. "Ugh." Jillian said with an eye roll. "I can't believe we might have to play them again."

A few of us started toward the bleachers so we could watch, but Mr. Letner called us back. "I'd prefer if you stayed in the hallway and didn't watch this game."

The Lazers players had all grabbed a ball and were firing them at the basket directly above our heads. "Assholes," Allan said under his breath.

Even though Mr. Letner had told us he thought we should stay in the hallway and ignore the game happening inside the gym, we kept sneaking to the gym doors to check the score. I was especially anxious to find out who won. If it was the Lazers, their coach might not let me play in the finals. After coming so far with my team, the thought of not being able to play in the championship game left a bitter taste in my mouth. Even if we weren't in the gym watching, it was obvious from the cheering that the fourth place team was no match for the Lazers. In the end, the Lazers won easily.

"Great," Jillian said sarcastically when she found out.

"Yesterday was a close game. We could have beat them," Mohammed said.

"They didn't let Sadia play," Mariam reminded everyone. "They'll do whatever it takes to win."

It was a long hour as we watched the team we'd beat in the semis play for third place. While everyone else sat in the bleachers chatting about school, the party, and our next game, I barely said a word. I had so many things to think about. Mainly, what would happen if the Lazers coach said I couldn't play? But Jillian's party was also weighing on my mind. I thought about how Mom had said high school could be a slippery slope. Mariam was definitely sliding: taking off her hijab, changing into gym clothes, and now roping me into lying so we could go to the party. My stomach churned and I stared at the court, willing myself to stay focused.

"Everyone ready?" Mr. Letner asked as the team gathered in the hall after the game. He sounded excited, which was good, because the butterflies in my stomach felt like they were caught in a hurricane. When no one answered him, he looked at us. "Why is everyone looking at me like that?" he asked. Finally, Jillian spoke. "I don't want to play if they don't let Sadia play." I gave her a sharp look.

"Yeah, me, too. If they pull that, we should all just leave," Allan agreed.

I started to shake my head, ready to argue that they *had* to play. This was the finals! We had to win and show the Lazers what a real team played like.

"I'm with Jillian and Allan. I don't want to play if they say no to Sadia," Josh said. He set his chin and gave me a determined look. I opened my mouth to argue, but there were more nods of agreement.

My stomach dropped as Mr. Letner looked at the circle of my teammates. "Does everyone feel that way?"

One by one, he met each player's eyes. One by one, they each nodded. Mr. Letner shook his head in disbelief. "I've never had a group of kids like you." His voice caught in his throat.

"You guys —" I started, ready to plead with them to play, no matter what. But he held up his hand.

"Your team has spoken, Sadia. And I couldn't be prouder." A swell of emotion rose in my chest. He stretched his arm into the middle of the circle and we piled our hands on top of it. "Three, two, one, Thunder!"

I didn't want my team to walk away from playing in the championship game, but I knew that if I'd been in their shoes, if someone had wanted to ban Jillian for playing because she had blond hair or Mohammed or Jeein because of their skin colour, I'd have stood up for them, too. One by one, my teammates and marched through the doors into the gym. Josh and I were the last two to leave.

Josh picked up his gym bag and put the strap over his head. He looked at me like he wanted to say something. "Josh —" I started.

"Sadia —" he said at the same time.

We broke off laughing. "I can't imagine playing without you," he said.

"We're good together," I agreed, meaning the whole team.

"Yeah, we are," he said. The look in his eye and the tilt of his mouth told me he meant something different.

I swallowed. "Josh —" I had to do it now. I couldn't keep pretending that something could happen between us, no matter how much I liked him. I could never date him; he would only ever be a friend. "My family has pretty strict rules about dating and stuff."

Josh's mouth turned down. "Yeah, Mo told me."

"Mohammed?" I choked back my surprise. "You asked him about it?"

"A while ago. I thought I should figure out if I had a shot or not."

"And what did he say?"

Josh shook his head and grinned at me. "That I didn't have one."

"So why —"

He shrugged. A blush crept up his neck and he turned away, embarrassed. He didn't have to say anything else. A warm glow filled me. Nothing was going to come of how I felt about Josh. I'd made that clear, but I couldn't stop him from liking me and I wasn't sure I even wanted to.

Our few minutes alone were interrupted by Mariam poking her head out of the gym doors. "It's almost game time! What are you two doing?" she asked.

"Nothing," I said.

"Making a game plan," Josh answered.

Mariam tilted her head, not believing either one of us. Josh walked past her and into the packed gym. "You shouldn't lie to your best friend," she whispered in my ear. *Best friend.* I hadn't heard her refer to me like that in a while.

"Tell you later," I promised. Because right now, I had a championship to win.

CHAPTER 25

Across the gym, the Lazers stretched and their coach eyed each player up and down, looking for weaknesses. "I'll go talk to the ref," Mr. Letner said, resolute.

I tried to keep my breathing even as I watched Mr. Letner walk across the floor. Mariam stood on one side of me and Jillian planted herself on the other. "Are you sure about this?" I asked. Letting the Lazers win would be a bitter pill to swallow.

"They'd win by default, which isn't really a win. And anyway, we're a team," she said with a grin. She picked up a ball and tossed it gently in the air. "I was talking with my mom yesterday about the passion project your class is doing. I was thinking, I'd like to do one, too."

"What would you do?"

"I want to see if I can get the rules changed about the uniform. You shouldn't have to choose between your religion and playing sports."

I looked at Jillian. Blond hair, blue eyed. The rule didn't affect her, would never affect her, but she was still willing to do something to change it, anyway. "That'd be amazing, Jillian."

The team quieted down and all eyes turned to watch Mr. Letner jog back to us with the answer from the Lazers coach. I squeezed my hands into fists, expecting the worst, but he gave us a thumbs-up.

"You can play!" came the excited voices of my teammates. A grin stretched across my face. Mariam and Jillian wrapped their arms around my shoulders and squeezed. I looked for Josh, a little ways away. He beamed at me.

Allan glared at the Lazers. Lou returned the look with a sneer. "They think they can beat us."

"But they can't." The determination I heard in my voice surprised even me.

Carmina, Riley, and a lot of other kids from 9B had made it to the game. They were sitting beside my parents and Mrs. Marino. I did a double take at the girl in hijab sitting behind her in the bleachers. Amira had come, too! She was sitting with her father. I waved at them and gave a thumbs-up. "I can play!" I shouted across the gym. Dad raised a fist in the air in celebration and Amira shouted good luck in Arabic.

Mr. Letner called us in for a team huddle and outlined our positions and plays. My palms were damp with nerves, but I ignored that and everything else to focus on what Mr. Letner had to tell us. "Remember, get aggressive. Don't be afraid to throw your body around. If this team is expecting us to lie down and let them walk all over us, they're wrong. We aren't going to let that happen, are we?"

"No!" we all shouted. "Three, two, one, Thunder!" The fans in the audience cheered as we took our positions on the court. Energy pulsed through me. My feet wanted to move and I couldn't wait to get the ball in my hands.

The first half of the game was back and forth. I'd been on the sidelines last time and had seen the aggressive play by the Lazers. Being on the court and feeling it was something else. Their elbows flew and they used their bodies to hip check and push us around. Twice, I collided with another player. We were all flushed and sweating by the half-time break and I was glad Mariam had sewn my uniform with light, athletic fabric. There was no way I could have played my hardest without it.

We went up by five points early in the second half and then Derek pushed Josh so hard he fell down and almost slid headfirst into the bleachers. There was an outcry from the stands. I could tell Josh was rattled. He didn't score on either of his foul shots, which got high-fives for Derek from his teammates. Unless we could convert the fouls into points, they'd keep playing dirty.

The play went back and forth. We'd score, then the Lazers would, until one of their players made a three-point shot and they went up on us by five points. With two minutes left in the game, Mr. Letner called a time out.

I looked at my parents and did another double take. Aazim was sitting beside them. He must have come in during the game and I hadn't noticed. He raised a hand and waved at me. I'd been so distracted by the game that I'd forgotten about last night. Everything rushed back. I looked at him again, but he didn't look mad. In fact, my parents and Aazim looked happy, like the tension from yesterday had disappeared. Were they pretending for my benefit, to keep me focused on the game, or had something changed?

"Sadia," Mr. Letner said, his voice sharper than usual. Everyone else was in the team huddle, paying attention, not gazing out into the stands. "Are you listening?"

Allan shuffled over to make room for me between him and Jillian. The next two minutes could win us the tournament.

Mr. Letner's face was flushed. His bald head shone under the gym lights and was covered by a thin sheen of sweat. "Jill, I'm putting you and Josh on the same line. I want you to do that play we practised on Thursday." Jillian nodded. Mr. Letner turned to Allan, his face intense. "You're going to get to the key and stay there. Don't let them rush you. Stand your ground. If they push you, push back. Sadia, get in as close to the basket as you can. If Allan can't make the shot, he'll pass to you. Take your time and set up the play. Ready?" He stuck out his hand and everyone piled theirs on top for the team cheer.

"Lazers!" we heard from the other side of the gym.

We ran into our positions. Josh got the play started. He dribbled the ball up the court and passed to Jillian; she moved back to centre and passed it to Allan. He faked and threw the ball to Josh, who drove into the key as if he was going for the shot. The Lazers centre moved in to block, but at the last second, Josh pivoted and threw the ball to me. I dribbled, boxing out the girl covering me, did a quick dash, and passed to Jill, who was out of the key. The Lazers were so confused, they didn't know who to cover. Jill shot and made three points. We were down by two. Allan grabbed the rebound to shoot again, but Lou, the Lazers player, shoved him so hard he fell to the floor with a thud. The ball rolled out of his hands and Lou grabbed it, ignoring the ref's whistle. He looked around with his hands spread wide. "What?" he asked, indignantly, as if it hadn't been an intentional foul.

I held out my hand to help Allan up. He glared with narrowed eyes at Lou and balled up his fists. "Wipe that smirk off your face, you piece of —" The ref blew his whistle and stood between Lou and Allan. I glanced at the bench. Mr. Letner shook his head, gritting his teeth. The ref passed the ball to Allan. "Two shots," he said.

Allan took his time moving to the foul-shot line. We all needed the breather. "Come on," I said under my breath. Everyone knew how important these two shots were. But we also knew that Allan was our weakest at sinking foul shots. He bounced the ball and took a deep breath. There was a lot of pressure on him. I was the player to his right, and when I caught his eye, I gave him a steely glare. He needed to focus. The first shot bounced off the rim. The Lazers fans cheered wildly. "You can do it, Allan!" I said, clapping. His teeth were clenched and I saw Lou scoff at him from under the basket. "Score this one for your brother," I said so quietly only he could hear me. Allan grinned and his shoulders relaxed. I inhaled as the basketball left his hands and sailed through the air. I didn't exhale until I heard the *swish* of the net and knew it had gone in. We were down by one!

The Lazers started their offence with even more aggression than before. Jillian tried to box their power forward, but he got past her, driving wide to the net. Josh came out of nowhere and jumped up to block the shot. It grazed his fingertips but it was enough of a deflection. The ball went wide and Thomas caught it. He ran it upcourt. "Over here!" Allan called. Thomas passed and Allan dodged both Lou and Derek, who collided with each other in their haste to get the ball. They both went down. Allan jumped over them. Three seconds left. He tossed the ball up just as the buzzer went. I held my breath. It went in! Final score: 51–50 for us!

The players on the bench and Mariam ran to the court, screaming. We jumped up and down, hugging and laughing. Mr. Letner walked on the floor high-fiving the team and trying to get us to line up to shake hands. It would have felt good to gloat, payback for all the unkind things the Lazers had said and done to our team. But Mr. Letner had been right. He'd told us to ignore their behaviour and focus on being a team. Well, we had and we'd won!

Some of the Lazers players had tears in their eyes and wouldn't look at us as we went down the line slapping hands. A chorus of "Good game. Good game" came from each of our players, but wasn't returned by the Lazers. Even the coach wouldn't look at Mr. Letner when it was their turn to shake hands. Mr. Letner walked away, shaking his head.

Both teams lined up for the trophy presentation and MVP award. Derek from the other team was called first. He came up to receive his certificate for MVP and shook hands with the coaches and ref. Next was the MVP award for our team. Because it was the finals, Mr. Letner made the pick. I crossed my fingers. Being named Most Valuable Player for the final game was a big deal. With Amira, Aazim, and my parents in the audience, I would have loved to hear my name over the sound system.

But it wasn't mine. It was Allan's. His mouth hung open as he stepped up to receive it. Mr. Letner shook his hand and clapped Allan on the shoulder. From the first row in the stands, Allan's mother stood up and hollered, "Way to go, Allan!" I looked over. She held out her phone, snapping a photo. Allan's brother sat beside her in his wheelchair. He couldn't clap, but the grin on his face said it all.

Then it was time to award the trophies. The tournament organizers came to the floor. Between them was the table with two awards on it. The finalist trophy went to the Lazers. But the big one, so tall it reached up to my waist, was for our team. It sparkled under the gym lights. "This year's JV All-City Basketball Tournament Champions are the Laura Secord Thunder!" Amidst lots of clapping, stamping, and hollering, our team captains, Jillian and Josh, were presented with the trophy. They stood with the organizers and let their parents take photos and then held it above their heads to more cheering. When Mr. Letner gave the signal, the rest of us rushed to them while parents crowded around to take a team photo.

"You should go in the middle, Allan. You're the MVP," Jillian said. She and Josh stood on either side and the rest of us crowded around, beaming. "Thunder!" we said as the parents held up their phones and snapped pictures.

Josh was standing beside me. His arm, casually draped across my shoulders, stayed there even after the photo shoot finished. "See you at the party, right?" he asked.

I nodded eagerly. Nothing could keep me away from celebrating our win. Mariam shot me an anxious glance; her eyes darted to just behind me. I turned and came face to face with my mom.

CHAPTER 26

I eased myself away from Josh and met Mom's penetrating glare. Josh and I had been way too close for her comfort. "What?" I asked innocently.

Her eyes flickered over to Josh, who had moved a few feet away to relive the game's best moments with Mohammed. Mom stared at me through her glasses, her mouth pulled tight with concern. "That boy —"

"He's just a friend." I lowered my voice, worried that someone would overhear.

Mom arched a skeptical eyebrow. "Really?"

But even as I nodded, a guilty blush crept up my cheeks. Mom turned her eyes to the ceiling, imploring a higher power. "What is happening to my children? One acting and this one hugging boys."

I had to roll my eyes, which was probably not the best choice. "It's not like that, Mom. You make it sound like —" I broke off, annoyed. At centre court, Mariam glanced my way. "Josh is my friend. That's it. *I promise.*"

Mom pursed her lips like she didn't believe me. "And the party? Why didn't you mention it before?"

"I forgot," I said lamely, and got the same dubious look. "I would have told you," I said with a sigh. "But Mariam —" I looked at my friend. "She knew if her parents found out, they wouldn't let her go."

"Why not?"

I crossed my arms over my chest. "You know how they are."

"So the sleepover you two were planning …" She let her question trail off and waited for me to confess.

"The whole team is invited, Mom! Mariam is part of the team. She should be allowed to go."

"That's not for you to decide." Her eyes narrowed suspiciously. "Whose house is the party at?"

My mouth twitched. Answering honestly would destroy Mariam's carefully constructed plan. I took a breath, ready to lie right to my mom's face. I opened my mouth to say "Ally's," but it was the truth that tumbled out. "Jillian's."

"Oh, Sadia." The disappointment in her voice made me cringe. It took all the shine off winning the tournament. "Who will be there to supervise? Her parents are away."

I hung my head, embarrassed at being caught in the lie.

"You know it isn't appropriate to for you to go to a party like that."

I bit the insides of my cheeks. A hot swell of disappointment rose up in my chest at the thought of not being able to celebrate with my team.

Mom sighed and shook her head. "There will always be these" — she hesitated, looking for the right word — "temptations. You and Mariam can't pick and choose which of our values you want to follow." Something about the way she said it made me wonder if she knew that from personal experience.

"The whole team is going. Mariam and I will be the only ones left out." I looked over at Jillian, Josh, Allan, Mohammed, and the rest of my team goofing around on the basketball court with the trophy. Mom followed my gaze. She'd seen first-hand what my team had been willing to sacrifice for my right to play. Hijab or no hijab, I was one of them. Kind of ironic that the thing they'd fought for was the same thing that would keep me from celebrating with them. "I can't not go, Mom," I said, my voice thick. She pursed her lips and shook her head. She didn't need to say anything. I could read the firmness of her answer on her face.

"Hey!" Jillian said as she bounded over, her phone out. "Can I get a picture of me and you with the trophy?" In a second, she realized she'd interrupted something tense and tried to make a hasty retreat. "Or maybe later —"

"Now is fine," Mom said with a thin-lipped smile and a pointed look in my direction. She left us, making a beeline for Dad and Aazim, who were talking with some other parents.

"Sorry, I didn't mean to interrupt," Jillian said.

"You weren't. We were just talking about the party —" I started. Jillian gave me an excited grin, making the next words even harder. "I can't go," I told her.

"Oh." Jillian's face fell. "Why not?"

I sighed, wishing I didn't have to explain.

Across the gym, I caught Mariam's eye and waved her over. "Is everything okay?" she asked.

I shook my head. "We can't go to Jillian's," I said. "Mom figured out what we were planning. And with your parents gone, she won't let us go to the party." I gave Jillian an apologetic look.

"That sucks," she said.

"It's my fault. She would have let you go if you hadn't tried to cover for me," Mariam said, glowering.

"No. I told her it was at Jillian's," I admitted. "She practically guessed anyway."

The three of us stood quietly for a minute, letting the news sink in. "So, it's not hanging out with the team that's the problem, it's that it's a party with no parents?" Jillian clarified.

I nodded, also thinking about the look on Mom's face when she saw Josh's arm draped across my shoulders. She hadn't been thrilled about seeing that either. "Basically."

Jillian's face brightened. "So they'd be cool if we went for a team dinner instead?"

I looked at Mariam. My parents would be and Mariam's probably would, too. We both nodded. Jillian spun around. "Team huddle!" she called.

As we were waiting for everyone to join us, Amira brought her father over to congratulate me. I felt like a celebrity the way he gushed about my play. It took away some of the sting about not being allowed to go to Jillian's party. "You are talented!" he said. "You have to teach Amira to play!"

I laughed and told him we were trying. The settlement worker who had driven them to the sportsplex commented on what an exciting game it was. Amira had filled him in on the drama surrounding my uniform.

"Sounds like I should be going to more high-school basketball games," he said, laughing.

"Thanks for coming," I said to Amira as they were leaving. "It means a lot to me." The smile she gave me was genuine, brighter and better than the trophy we'd won.

Jillian had corralled the team, including Mr. Letner. "Who's in for a team dinner at the restaurant next door?"

It wasn't the same as a party, but at least we'd get to celebrate as a team, the same way we'd played.

Everyone nodded.

"And then the party at your house?" Allan asked.

"I don't think everyone can make it," Jillian explained. I cast a quick glance at Mariam. "This time. But maybe next weekend, when my parents are home, we can have one that is *exclusive*. Just us." She grinned at Mariam and me.

"Sounds good!"

"Thanks, Jillian," I whispered to her as the team dispersed.

There was no telling if Mariam would be able to go to that party or not, but at least she had a week to come up with a convincing argument for her parents. And if anyone could do it, it was Mariam.

"Hey, it's the latest in hijabi fashion!" Aazim said with a grin as I joined the group of parents and kids making their way toward the exit doors. "That was a great game," he said. "Your team is really good!"

"Thanks." I smiled at him. "I'm glad you made it."

"Me, too." Aazim didn't seem mad at me. Was he just being nice, not wanting to tarnish my post-win glow? Or were we really okay? I gave him a puzzled look, hoping for an explanation.

"We have two winners in our family!" Dad exclaimed. "This one for basketball and look at this." Dad held a copy of the newspaper he'd brought from home. "Right here in the entertainment section." A photo of Aazim onstage with the headline "No Dark Days for Star of University Play."

I looked at Aazim and he gave me a wide smile. "A four-star review. Dad's been getting phone calls from friends who saw the review all day."

"So maybe Aazim should keep acting." I raised an eyebrow at my parents.

"We'll see. Studies come —"

"First," Aazim and I said together. "We know."

CHAPTER 27

The gallery hosting the school's art show was downtown, in an old brick warehouse. As we climbed the stairs to the second floor, a sign caught my eye. "If You Give a Kid a Camera Photo Exhibit: Life from the Perspective of the Grade Nine Students, Laura Secord High School." Floor-to-ceiling windows bathed the space in light. The gallery used to be a garment factory and there were still remnants of its previous life. An old sewing machine sat in one corner, with a photograph of the immigrant women who'd worked here. I'd looked at that photo for a long time yesterday, when we'd had a sneak preview of our exhibit, wondering what it had been like for those women to move to Canada and how different, or not so different, their story was from mine. They'd have faced boundaries and discrimination, too, as they made their way in a new country.

Art from lots of students at Laura Secord was on display: paintings done in oil, acrylic, and watercolour, and sketches. But it was our photos, enlarged and framed, hung on the white walls of the gallery that I was most interested in. I knew the story behind each one, what the photo meant to the person who had taken it, and why they had chosen it to go on display.

Mr. Letner had asked us to include a typed write-up giving some background on the photo. They hung on the wall beside each photograph and included the student's name and the photo's title.

It was the first evening that the exhibit was open to the public and a lot of kids had come to show their parents around. Mom, Dad, and I kicked the snow off our boots on the mat at the entrance. Mom had come from her new part-time job as head librarian of the Arabic section at the Millennium Library. She hadn't let the attitude of the woman at the bus stop or the guy in the truck get to her. In fact, I think it had pushed her to apply.

She'd come home her first week and proudly showed us a stack of business cards with her name and title on them. "I never thought it would be possible!" she'd cried giddily. Most nights, she poured over catalogues, looking for books to add to the library and sending out emails to encourage Arabic speakers to join her for book clubs and language lessons. She was making her way in Canada, too, maybe not as quickly as Dad had, but she was finding a path on her own, just like Aazim and I were.

The hardwood floors creaked under our footsteps as I brought my parents over to my photograph. In the end, I hadn't chosen a photo of basketball at all. I'd picked one I'd taken the day Amira and I went tobogganing. I'd taken it standing off to the side, halfway up the hill as Amira sped down on the red sled. The skeletal trees behind the hill were silhouetted against the cloudy sky. She was laughing, her mouth open wide as snowflakes fell around her, the red sled bright against the white snow. The card beside it read:

> My friend Amira tobogganing for the first time. She is a Syrian refugee and I like how this photo shows how happy she can be. Hopefully, how happy she will be. She's had a lot of tragedy in her life, but I hope now that she's in Canada, she'll be able to have more days filled with laughter.
> — Sadia Ahmadi

I led Mom and Dad through the exhibit, pointing out the photographs I wanted them to see and giving them the backstory. They stayed for a while looking at the one of Allan carrying his brother.

Carmina's photo was in black and white: a bunch of our hands stacked one on top of the other, thumbs interlocking, the shades a flesh-toned rainbow. She'd titled it *Class 9B*. I found my hand right away, nestled under Josh's and on top of Mariam's.

Beside us, Josh stood with his parents in front of the picture he'd chosen. It was the one of his dad standing at the glass, yelling at his brother. I wondered if Josh had shown it to him before or if this was the first time he'd seen it. Josh stared at his dad unapologetically. "Do I really look like that?" his dad asked.

A flicker of doubt crossed Josh's face, as if he was hesitating in giving an honest answer. "Yeah, you do."

"Look at this one!" Mom exclaimed as we moved

through the gallery. "That's you at the tournament!" Mariam, unbeknownst to me, had taken a photo of me as the crowd had chanted, "Let her play!" I got shivers looking at it, remembering that moment when I realized the whole gymnasium was sticking up for me. In the photo, my eyes were filled with tears as I stared at the crowd. The expression on my face was hard to explain: part awe, part gratitude, and part disbelief. I loved that it had been Mariam who had captured that moment. It was because of her that I'd been able to play at all.

My parents stared at the photo, the moment as special for them as it was for me.

They leaned toward the card on the wall. I didn't need to read it; I'd almost memorized the words. It was titled: *One for the Team.*

> I sewed the outfit for Sadia to wear at a basketball tournament. She's a Muslim teenager who almost wasn't allowed to play in a tournament game because the outfit didn't meet the rules of what's considered appropriate for basketball. The whole gymnasium, even the other team, stood up for her right to play. This photo was taken just before she found out she'd be able to play.
> — Mariam Hassanin

But the photos I was most excited to show them were Amira's. Mr. Letner had let her display a series of photographs. Through her camera lens, we got to see what *she* did — her perspective as a refugee in Canada. Miss McKay had helped with the write-ups, but I could hear Amira's voice in the words. The first photo was of the cereal aisle at a grocery store. Row upon row of brightly coloured cereal boxes, more than we needed, stacked neatly and ready to be consumed. After eating hand to mouth for so long, the abundance of food had left her speechless the first time she saw it. I'd never thought about the grocery store before, about how much we had in Canada — food, stuff, everything — but Amira did. I'd never known real hunger, but Amira had. How could I ever throw around the words *I'm starving* again? Mom and Dad leaned away from the card on the wall and looked at the photo.

Another photo showed her four brothers, squished together, asleep in her bed. Beside them, the bunk beds lay empty.

> My brothers prefer to sleep together even though they have bunk beds. After spending so much time in the camps, they don't like to sleep apart.

"It's powerful to hear about the photos in her words," Dad said.

The next photo was of Amira's parents, sitting side by side on the couch at their apartment. They had the cell phone between them; Mr. Nasser was holding it up so they could both hear the speaker. They weren't looking into the camera, but their faces were contorted with grief. Unchecked tears slid down her father's face. It was a candid moment, maybe too personal. I hoped they weren't mad at Amira for capturing it.

> My parents on the phone to our family in Syria. They have found out my uncle was killed. He had no children and stayed behind to look after my grandparents. Now, they are alone.

Teachers, parents, and other students paraded through the gallery. Mr. Letner had set up a schedule so we'd all get a turn to act as a guide, explaining the project and taking people through the exhibit. There was also a silver collection plate for people to leave money, like a *zakat* at the mosque. As a class, we'd taken a vote on where to donate the money.

We'd learned a lot this semester in Mr. Letner's class. As he walked around, talking to kids and their parents, I realized how lucky we were to have him as our teacher. He could have protected us from the world, hiding the ugly truths, but he wanted us to expose them, face them head on, and challenge them. My time in his class was one I'd never forget.

CHAPTER 28

Outside the classroom windows, icicles dripped. Spring was itching to break through and winter was almost behind us. With March break around the corner, I was looking forward to playing basketball in the driveway with Aazim — or maybe Jillian, or even Josh.

I looked out at my class. It was my turn to present my passion project. A map of the world was on the screen behind me. I looked out at Amira, and Mariam beside her. Carmina gave me an encouraging smile. Mariam had continued to make an effort with Amira, sitting with her at lunch if I had to leave for basketball, or translating for her so she could follow conversations. Some days Mariam wore her hijab and some days she didn't. I'd stopped worrying about it. Mariam was who she was.

"The countries with the red circles" — I pointed with my finger at the circles in the Middle East, Africa, Central America, Asia, and Eastern Europe — "are the original homes of today's refugees. The United Nations says there are sixty million refugees in our world."

Next, I put up the photo Amira had shown us of her friends at the track meet. "This semester, I've learned how important my friends are to me. There are a lot of things that I couldn't have done without them." I looked at the kids from the basketball team, my eyes lingering on Mariam. "When Amira came to our class, I didn't know that much about refugees, even though I was from Syria. My relatives left before the war got really bad. Most of them live in the U.K. We were lucky. If we hadn't left, if my dad hadn't got his job at the university when he did, we might have *had* to leave, like Amira did. We might have been refugees, too." I looked around the classroom. "One of the things I think would be the hardest about being a refugee is losing your friends and family. Not knowing where they are, if they are even still alive." I showed an aerial image of a refugee camp in Lebanon. Dingy cloth tents stretched for kilometres. "I wanted to do something to help Amira find her friends, so I did some searching and found an organization called RefUnite." I clicked to the next slide.

"RefUnite.org helps refugees find their friends and family." I showed them how to navigate the page. "This is where Amira's family signed up. They put in their contact information and the names of the people they are trying to locate. When those people sign up, RefUnite.org will notify Amira's family. Helping Amira's family got me thinking that other people are going through the same thing. I got in touch with the Immigrant and Refugee Community Organization of Manitoba." I pulled up a screen shot of the organization's home page. "IRCOM is a non-profit organization that operates a transitional housing complex in downtown Winnipeg. The residents have access to services like driver's ed courses, English language classes, and homework clubs, and they help newcomers figure things out, like banking and child care.

"When I emailed the program director, she said she hadn't heard about RefUnite, so she invited me down to talk about it." I showed a slide of me in front of a group of people; two women wearing brightly patterned African dresses and head wraps, three Somali women, and a Syrian family. "A lot of the people who came to my presentation don't have access to the internet, so I helped them enter their information." The next picture showed me at a laptop with a woman named Zebiba sitting beside me. She'd left Somalia a year ago and had lost touch with her family.

I looked out at my class and at Mr. Letner. "I'm going back next week to meet with another group of refugees."

I smiled at Amira. "So far, we haven't had any luck finding Amira's friends, but it's only been a week. I'm going to keep monitoring it for her family and let them know if anyone tries to contact them. Any questions?"

Josh raised his hand. "So if it works, and you find someone, how do they connect? You said a lot of people don't have computers."

"RefUnite lets you choose the way you want to connect with people. It can be by texting, messaging, Facebook, or a land line.

"The other thing that made all of this tricky was that no one really speaks English. They're all learning, so there were lots of hand gestures." I thought about Amira and how much she'd learned since she arrived. I looked around the class, but no one else's hand went up. "I guess I'll keep you posted and let you know if we hear from any of Amira's friends." I put the photo of the girls back up on the screen. The Amira sitting before me now looked more like the one in the photo with the crinkled, laughing eyes and bright smile. "And Mr. Letner wanted me to tell you that he counted our votes about where to donate money and the Red Cross won. We'll donate the silver collection from the exhibit to help other refugees." There were lots of nods of agreement.

Mr. Letner came to the front of the classroom. "Thanks, Sadia." The class clapped for me as I went back to my seat. "You know, all of this started with 'If You Give a Kid a Camera,'" he said thoughtfully. "And since the semester began, you've all done something to change to the world around you. Allan made a tool for his brother to use so he can operate the remote control on his own; Franca made a cookbook with her grandmother's recipes and sold it at school to raise money. She's decided to add to our Red Cross donation."

I turned and grinned at Franca. She gave me a proud smile in return. "Josh is working with Jillian Triggs to get the All-City tournament to change the uniform rules." Mariam nudged me with her elbow. Once Josh had heard what Jillian was doing, he'd wanted to help, too. The two of them had been collecting signatures and going to classrooms to talk about human rights and why no one should be barred from playing a sport because of their religious beliefs. Mr. Letner smiled at us. In the end, almost everyone had chosen to do a passion project. "I've never had a Global Issues class like you kids before. You make me proud to be your teacher."

I swallowed back a lump in my throat. "If you give a kid a teacher …" I whispered.

"She'll want to learn," Mariam added, with a smile.

"And if she wants to learn …" Amira continued quietly.

"She'll want to change the world."

AUTHOR'S NOTE

The If You Give a Kid a Camera project is fictional, but it was inspired by 100Cameras, a project which operates on the same principles as the one described in the book. Check it out at www.100cameras.org.

RefUnite is a real organization that reunites refugees with loved ones. If you would like more information, go to their website at www.refunite.org.

IRCOM is also a real organization based in Winnipeg. More information about the work it does for newcomers to Canada can be found at www.ircom.ca.

ACKNOWLEDGEMENTS

I could not have written this book without the help of Nadia Kidwai. She read the manuscript, provided feedback, and ensured I was on the right path. She continued to help by answering many questions throughout the editing process. Thank you, Nadia! This book wouldn't have been possible without you.

Thank you to Cindy Kochanski for her always insightful comments. Thank you also goes to Owen Kochanski for reading the book and providing encouraging comments. I am always grateful for the support of my family: my sisters, Nancy and Karen, for watching my kids so I could write; my mom for instilling in her children the confidence and security to take chances; and my husband, Sheldon, who has forced me to watch many college basketball games over the years (Go Zags!). Thank you to my boys, James and Thomas, for answering basketball-related questions and for backing slowly out of the room when they saw I was *still* working on the book.

The lovely people at Dundurn continue to make publishing with them a wonderful experience. A huge thank you to Carrie Gleason for accepting the book;

Kathryn Lane, Jenny McWha, and Catherine Dorton, who made sure it was the best it could be; Ashley Hisson for proofreading; Naila Alidina for her insights; and Laura Boyle, who designed the interior and created the striking cover.

Part of the inspiration for this book came from teaching students new to Canada. I am always amazed, not just at the speed with which they acquire a new language, but at their ability to adapt and settle into a new culture. It was my intention to write a book that reflected their experiences and to show other readers the challenges, and triumphs, that accompany moving to a new country.

As a writer, my goal is to create characters with unique voices. I believe writing is about taking risks and doing what Mr. Letner implores his class to do with their photos: show a new perspective. Through writing, and reading, we gain empathy and understanding of others. *Sadia* is a book about friendship, acceptance, and standing up for your rights. With all my heart, I hope it reaches an audience of readers who are open-minded and believe in the power of the student voice.